The Secret Service of Angels

Tex
To one
author
from
another!
Love & Peace
Mary

Mary 'Fig' Stearne

ISBN 978-1-63844-893-8 (paperback)
ISBN 978-1-63844-894-5 (digital)

Christian Faith Publishing, Inc.
832 Park Avenue
Meadville, PA 16335
www.christianfaithpublishing.com

Printed in the United States of America

It was not you who chose me, but I who chose you and appointed you to go and bear fruit that will remain, so that whatever you ask the Father in my name he may give you. This I command you: love one another.

—John 15:16–17

I am dedicating this story to all our *fallen heroes*—those who gave their lives in the battle for our freedom and the heroes who were never on the battlefield. This is also for our families that teach our children right from wrong and that keep alive all the traditions and stories of our history. Lastly, this story is for all who protected our faith, values, and freedom.

No one has greater love than this, to lay down one's life for one's friends.

—John 15:13

CONTENTS

Chapter 1

Divine Intervention

"These photos are awesome, Mom! Did Grandmom take all of them?" Maria Thompson questioned her mother in the photo gallery at Saint Albans, Maine.

Gloria Thompson replied, "Yes! And it's hard to believe it's been eight years since her death."

Maria was only fifteen when her grandparents passed away. They said it was an accidental death. She always thought it was foul play, but of course, no one would listen to a fifteen-year-old. She was determined to prove them wrong.

That's what inspired her to pursue a career in forensics. But she also knew it was going to take more than forensics; she also wanted to get into the mind of a criminal. She was selected to go into the Naval Academy to study law. Now, she is a Second Lieutenant in the Marines and taking a course in forensics.

Her grandfather, Tobit Wright, was involved in the Criminal Investigation Command (CID). Guess one could say that she was a chip off the old block.

Maria used to listen to many stories from her grandpop. They would often spend hours watching unsolved mysteries together. He supposedly retired from the CID, but she had this feeling that one investigation had never been solved. She wanted to dedicate her life to solving this eight-year-old mystery.

"Grandmom Sarah would be pleased to know that your father and I are going to visit their home in Fredericksburg, Virginia." Gloria whispered.

Maria acknowledged her with a nod as they left the gallery.

"I've been waiting forever for you, girls," Joseph Thompson exaggerated a little.

He was waiting for only five minutes.

"You know little Maria had to stop and see my mother's photo exhibits," Gloria said, ratting her out.

Although Maria's grandparents' house was in Fredericksburg, Virginia, their hearts were in Saint Albans, Maine where they planned to retire. Maria had many fond memories of Maine. Sarah would get her up very early in the morning so she could capture her nature photography.

"Quiet, little Maria! You have to be very still and patient to get the perfect picture," she would tell her because she was always asking questions.

"Okay, Grandmom, not a peep out of me…"

"Look, little one! There is a buck in the field. Don't breathe," she would whisper as she clicked the camera shutter and captured the perfect shot.

"You are a good assistant. I don't know what I'd do without you."

"Well, we have a long ride to Virginia. Do you remember any of the car songs that we used to sing when you were little?"

Joseph had to keep Maria's attention off the driving when she was younger because she always got car sick. So they sang songs and played car games like I Spy or "100 bottles of sodas on the wall" (it should have been "beers on the wall," but she was young, and her dad thought sodas would be appropriate). He continued, "We will make a stop halfway in New Jersey. The rates are cheaper at the hotels this time of the year."

"That sounds like a great idea, Joseph. Now you can lead us in a song." Gloria laughed.

Her parents decided that it was time to sell her grandparents' house in Fredericksburg. They haven't been there since the "accident." Sarah and Tobit were trying to do the same thing eight years ago but, unfortunately, never had a chance to. They worked as a team and retired as a team. He was in the Marines for ten years and joined the CID in Quantico, Virginia. And, of course, Sarah would take photos of many crime scenes. It wasn't her full-time job. She worked for *National Geographic* magazine, but that was a part-time job too. Even though she loved nature photography, she also liked being involved in solving mysteries, just like her husband.

"I hope Maria remembers the stories Tobit told her about us."

"I think she does, Joe. We are the fallen heroes."

"Yep, we won many battles because many of us believe the freedom of the *way*: the way of truth and justice. The war Tobit was in almost cost him his life. We would have won that one too if so many fallen heroes "believed what they were fighting for."

"You are so right, Joe. We had so many who sacrificed themselves for one another in the two world wars. Our servicemen were many and strong, and victory was ours. Well, we still have other battles to fight. I hope Robert can make contact with Maria. She did promise to solve the mystery of her grandparents' death."

"She sure did."

They finally made the halfway point to Virginia. If Maria had to sing about one more soda on the wall, she thought she would go crazy. They then checked into a bed and breakfast at Ocean City, New Jersey. Now they can relax and watch the sunset on the bay.

"Come on, sleepyhead! Time to wake up for breakfast and get on our way. It's your turn to drive the rest of the way. Are you up for it?" Gloria announced as though Maria had a choice.

Maria murmured, "Yes, I know: Give me five minutes."

She wasn't looking forward to returning to the unpleasant memory of losing her loving grandparents. No, she didn't forget her promise to find out what really happened that day on the lake.

It was a long drive, but they all arrived safe and sound. They were also hungry and tired. After settling in, they went out to eat at their favorite diner, Masello's Italian Diner. Maria's grandmom and Maria would often go there, and it was just the two of them. They were like best friends with best-friend secrets.

"Hello! Is this little Maria?" Said Paula, their waitress. "You have grown into a beautiful young lady."

"Yes, she is," her mom said, putting in her two cents, "and it is not just because she is my daughter. She looks like her grandmom."

"Why, thank you, guys. I'm proud of that, but grandmom Sarah has me beat when it comes to looks."

"Is your grandmom's sister Jean coming down too?" Inquired Paula.

"She is taking care of the gallery back in Maine," Maria replied. But she knew she couldn't handle seeing the place where her sister had her accident. She was there when it happened and was having a very hard time getting on with her life. Her husband had died a year before the tragedy.

"Well, ladies, time to go back to the house and get some rest. We have a lot of work tomorrow."

Joseph was right about that; they had to fix the house up so they can sell it. But that wouldn't happen until Maria investigated what happened there.

*****

"Maria," someone whispered, "Maria." She awoke from her sleep.

There was no one there. She could have been dreaming, but it sounded so real as if someone was right in her room.

There was a tapping sound at the window. She walked to the window and heard someone calling her name.

"Maria? It's me, Robert."

"Robert! What are you doing here so late at night?"

"Please come down. We have to talk, and I don't have much time," he responded.

Robert McDaniel was only fourteen years old when Maria last saw him, and she wasn't sure if she could recognize him if she saw him again. He did go to the same school as her, but he was a year younger than her. His parents had a vacation house next to her grandparents' house.

Sarah and Tobit had some unexpected business come up, and Maria remembered that they asked the neighbors if she could stay with them. It wasn't too unusual for her to stay with them because she and Robert were close friends, and she often stayed overnight at their place. But she would never forget that night—it was the last time she ever saw her grandparents alive.

They both swore to each other when they were older that they were going to find out what really happened; they knew it was no accident. The last thing she heard about him was that he joined the Marines and was deployed to Afghanistan.

"What is Robert doing here? He is not supposed to contact Maria until tomorrow."

"You are right, Joe. Something is wrong, and we don't have time to alert Michael. We have to intervene before she gets to the door."

The fallen hero didn't have as much power over the fallen angel as the original angels, but he had many years of practice.

The light from the back porch shone on the young man's face, and Maria should see him from her window.

"Okay, Rob, I will be right down," she said.

"Oh yes, that's a good girl, Maria. Come down to see your Robert," a sinister voice blurted out in the night.

*****

Alexander, a hero who fought in the Korean War in the 1950s, was killed saving his platoon. He knew he would die for his troops. He was welcomed to join the "special secret service" to fight for the freedom of all mankind. Tonight, he was there, staring down at the fallen angel Azza.

Azza looked intensely at the door with his amber-colored eyes waiting for Maria. He did not notice Alexander.

"Be gone from this place, demon! You cannot stop Maria from her destiny," commanded Alexander.

"And who are you to speak with such authority?" Azza questioned him.

"I have been anointed by the Archangel Michael as the Commander of the *Fallen Heroes*," replied Alexander.

Azza cried out with a chilling scream, "You haven't seen the last of me, Commander!" He fled into the dark of the night knowing he had no power over him.

Maria heard what sounded like thunder and was frightened. But knowing Robert was there, she opened the back door to see him. Before she could touch the door handle, a gust of wind blew it open. She had flown across the room and was knocked unconscious.

Alexander carried her to her room and laid her down on her bed. "You will have a little headache tomorrow, Maria, but you will believe you only had a bad dream."

*****

"Maria? Maria, wake up. Breakfast is ready," called her mother.

Oh boy, do I have a headache? What a strange dream I had last night; it seemed so real! She thought. "Okay, Mom, I'll be right down," Maria answered. "Why are you guys up so early?"

Her Father replied, "You and I have to go into town and get some supplies so we can get this house in shape. You will go to the department store and get some stuff on this list your mother made, and I will go to the hardware store and try to find some contractors to do some jobs we can't handle ourselves."

"Okay, Dad. Good breakfast, Mom."

"Yes, it sure was dear," Maria and her daddy flattered Gloria.

"You better get going, guys. I'll clean up here."

Gloria didn't want them to waste time; she just wanted to get the ball rolling.

"Okay, little Maria, let's get going. Here's your mom's list," Joseph was giving the orders, as usual.

They finally made it to their destination. Maria had her list and told her dad she will call him when she was finished. Joseph agreed, and he headed for the hardware store.

*****

They were being watched from the parking lot. Two demonic fallen angles were getting ready to stop Maria from meeting Robert today.

But this time, Michael the Archangel was present to make sure they wouldn't interfere. He gave the command: "You have no power here! Be gone!"

"Yesss, we don't have the power, but we'll be back with our leader, Apollyon, to get what we came for."

Before they could vanish, Michael raised his hand and banished them to hell. Now they couldn't report to their leader.

*****

In the corner of Maria's eye, she saw someone looking her way.

"Maria, Maria?"

She turned to see who it was.

"Hello, Maria. It's me, Robert. Do you remember me? It's been a long time… And a long time coming."

This time, it wasn't a dream; it really was Robert McDaniel.

"Is it really you?" She asked with concern in her voice.

"It's me, Robert; it is great to see you again. How long has it been, about seven or eight years?"

"Oh, Robert! It's good to see you. It has been eight years. And just last night, I had a vivid dream that you were at my grandparents' back door."

She still couldn't believe that it was a dream. She could still feel the arms of someone carrying her to her bedroom.

"What brings you here? I heard you joined the Marines and were deployed to Afghanistan. No one told me you were home yet."

"We made a promise to each other, and I'm here to keep that promise. Can we meet tonight at our secret place when we were younger?"

I don't know if I can get away without my parents questioning me, she thought to herself. *They still think it was an accident. And they don't even want me to pursue or even talk about it anymore.*

"Is that why you didn't tell anyone you were in town? I won't let anyone know I have seen you, if you want."

"Yes, please don't let anyone know you saw me," answered Robert. "But I am here for only a short amount of time."

She replied, "Okay, how about seven o'clock? I will make some excuse after dinner to my mom and dad." Looking away for a second, Maria turned back to look at Robert, but he was gone.

Oh no, was she really talking to him or not? Well, she will find out tonight at seven.

Chapter 2

SECRET HIDEAWAY

She finished her shopping and got all the stuff on her mom's list. She hoped she could get out of the house without her parents asking her too many questions. *I better call Dad to see if he is ready*, she said to herself.

"Hey, Dad! I'm finished with my list. Do you want me to meet you at the hardware store?" Maria asked.

"Okay, Maria. I'd like you to meet two of mine and mom's friends. You might remember them from when you were little. Their names are Ruth and Peter Grossman. They asked us to come to dinner tonight and stay over."

"Well, I'll see you in a few minutes. But I won't go with you to your friends' house. I have some things to work on before I have to go back to my base."

She had to think of some excuse. *Even though I have three weeks leave, I still have to do my studies on my computer. So that excuse was believable.* Time was of the essence, and Maria only had less than three weeks to get to the bottom of this mystery.

*****

Back in the veterans' hospital at Quantico, a serviceman hanging on for dear life was guarded by the heroes who didn't make it back safely from the explosion in Afghanistan. But they were selected by Michael to keep him safe from the evil lurking in the lower floor of the building. It was not the serviceman's time to be called into the Special Secret Service of Angels. His job was to stay alive to protect our nation and its future.

One of the new recruits was the injured young man's best friend, Sam. Sam was a few years younger than the injured Marine; he was only nineteen years old. Not only was he too young to give up his life but also he was a greenhorn in this Special Secret Service. So he was quite naive about what would happen next.

Sam was at the end of his friend's bed keeping watch when he heard someone calling his name. He thought it could be Michael the Archangel.

"Sam, come here; your post has been changed."

"Michael, is that you? I am the only one watching at the doorway. I will not leave my post," Sam replied.

The impostor commanded Sam with his demanding voice, "Someone will take your place. Leave your post!"

Sam started to step toward the door when he suddenly remembered what Michael told him and the other: "If you are told to change your post, you must always address whoever is giving you these different orders by saying the name of the Most High: 'Jesus.' If the angel is from us, he will not flee. If he is not from us, he will tremble with fear."

Just then, he saw a shadow that was ready to take his place. Sam shouted the name Jesus. At that moment, an awful cry came out of the fallen one; and he vanished.

"My God, I am so sorry. Michael would be disappointed with me."

Michael suddenly appears in the room to speak with Sam. "You have done a brave job protecting your friend. I need you and Gabriel to go to Sarah and Tobit's estate. Maria will be meeting Robert tonight, and I know the fallen ones will be there to stop her," he ordered.

"Oh no, not I, Michael, I am not ready. I almost lost my best friend to our enemy," replied Sam.

"You are a humble servant. Your heart is ready." Michael anointed Sam and sent him on his way.

He remained with the injured young man until a replacement hero came to guard him.

*****

Joseph and Maria were heading home. "Did you ask Mom yet about going to see your friends tonight?" asked Maria. "Yes, she was fine with it. But I was really hoping you would change your mind. I think your mom would be disappointed too," replied Joseph.

"What took you two so long? Did you get everything on my list? And I hope you got a good contractor," Gloria said.

"I got everything on your list."

"And I got a few offers. We can go over them together and see who is most qualified for the job."

She was happy with their answers.

Maria headed to her room to rest before meeting with Robert tonight. She wanted to tell her parents, but they would ask too many questions. Besides, Robert told her not to say anything.

"Maria, your father and I are ready to go now. Are you sure you don't want to come with us?" Her mom asked.

"Please, Mom, you just go. I really have to stay and get things done. I have to take my final exams when I get back to my base, and I want to make sure I ace them."

"Come on, Gloria, leave her be. She's a big girl now, and she knows what's best for her," interrupted Joseph.

Maria confirmed, "Yes, Mom and Dad. You have a great time."

*****

Robert got to the meeting place early...and so did a dark creature lurking around and looking for clues. The fallen angels needed to find these clues so they could stop what Sarah and Tobit started. They somehow crossed over while a few fallen angels were trying to retrieve a special satellite that was not known to anyone on earth.

When Tobit was alive, he could still communicate with the fallen heroes from time to time. That was because he died while on a mission and was brought back to life. But when he left his body, he had several encounters with his guardian angel and other spiritual beings.

The Archangel Gabriel and Sam were headed to Sarah and Tobit's estate. Michael had caught up to them with a change in plans.

"Gabriel and Sam, do not go to the secret hideaway. There is something I must take care of first. Robert will need you tonight. You keep watch here until I send for you." He then rushed to protect Robert from another demon that was trying to prevent him from seeing Maria.

"I will have to try and get rid of that Robert before Maria gets here," contemplated the lowly creature.

As he readied himself to go after Robert, Michael intervened. "You have no power over me, demon. Be gone!"

Robert turned around and saw the creature in flames and fleeing with a loud cry.

"What was that? Who is there?"

Michael was not sure if Robert had seen him, so he quickly hid himself behind the trees. But Robert did see him and wondered if he should tell Maria about this when he meets her.

"I saw you go behind the tree. Please show yourself?"

"You can see me, Robert?"

"Yes, who are you? And why was that creature you sent away running?" Robert asked Michael.

Michael came out from behind the trees. "I am Michael the Archangel. You and Maria will find out what happened to Sarah and Tobit but don't tell her about what you have seen tonight. That creature wanted to stop you both."

Robert sighed to himself. "She would never believe me, anyway."

*****

Maria's parents had finally left. Now she was getting ready to leave and meet up with Robert. She wondered why no one said anything about Robert being in town. And he didn't even want her to tell her parents. She was hoping he finds their secret place because it has been so long.

Maria thought she better get going. Her grandmom's secret place is about an acre from the house. That place was a secret from everyone but her. Grandmom Sarah told her that grandpop Tobit built it just for her to do her work with her magic camera. That was what Grandpop called it. The only person Maria did share it with was Robert. He was so into photography, and Sarah shared some of her secret tips. She was his adopted grandmom, and he loved her so. That is why he is so determined to find out the truth.

*****

Robert was eagerly waiting for Maria. He heard a rustling near their special tree where they carved their initials and their promise to always be friends.

"Maria is that you?" He asked but not too loudly because he was afraid it might be the creature he saw earlier.

After a long pause, a voice replied, "It's me, Maria. Is that you, Robert?"

With a sigh of relief, Robert spoke up, "Yes, I'm here. I'm so glad it's you!"

"Who else would it be? This is our secret spot."

Robert wasn't about to tell her who else knew of their secret spot.

They headed toward the house and went in the same direction while looking for the front door key.

"You still remember where it's hidden?" she asked him.

"Yes, I do. I'm surprised I remember."

They reached for the door but found that it was already open. Was there someone inside?

"Looks like someone was here, but they did not use our key."

Maria touched Robert's shoulder. "Let's go in the back way. If someone is still in there, we can surprise them."

Yes, there was someone, but while Robert was waiting for Maria, Michael took care of him before he could find what he came for.

"Okay, Maria. But whoever was here probably heard us and fled."

"You think someone who knows what happened that night knows I'm in town?" questioned Maria.

"No, I think everyone here was convinced it was an accident," said Robert. "Perhaps you're right. Let's go in and see if the place looks okay."

*****

"Okay, deadbeat. Did you find any clues that would lead Maria and Robert to where the box is?" asked Shea, the fallen angel in charge.

"No, the Archangel Michael showed up. And you know we have no powers to defeat him," answered the fallen angel.

Shea was furious. He pounced on him and threw him across the field. "I guess I have to go myself before the boss finds out!" he bellowed.

*****

Maria and Robert went through the back way and found the door wide open. Indeed, someone was there and made a mess of things. There was black soot everywhere.

"What does this mean? You think someone knew we were coming?" questioned Maria.

Robert wondered if he should tell her about what he witnessed before she arrived even if he initially said he wouldn't. Maybe if he did tell her, she would share with him what she thought was a dream.

Maria went to the fireplace where she knew of a secret hiding place. "Yes, the key to her darkroom is still here. She had two darkrooms. Grandmom Sarah let me look in there only once. She told me that someday, when I am older, she would show me why this darkroom was hidden." Her eyes began to fill with tears; she wished her grandmom was there to see her now and share her secret.

Robert touched her shoulder to give her comfort. "Maria, before you look inside the room, I have to tell you what happened before you arrived. I was told not to tell you, but I think you should know given the circumstance.

"There was someone or something here tonight trying to stop me from meeting with you. Then an angel-like man vaporized the creature. When I asked him what happened and who he was, he told me he was Michael, the Archangel. He was surprised that I could see him, and he told me not to tell you. Marie, you probably think I'm crazy now, but it really happened. Michael did say that we will find out what happened to your grandparents, but we are not alone. There is another force trying hard to stop us."

Wow, I feel like a fool after blurting that out. She will just think I need help from a shrink, he thought.

"My grandfather told me stories about the fallen heroes. But I thought they were just stories; some were really frightening. The battles between good and evil are real, Robert, aren't they?"

Maria thought about her dream. She was beginning to have second thoughts about that. She decided to tell Robert her story too.

"I had a haunting dream last night. You were calling me into the backyard while I was in my bedroom. When I went out to meet you, someone pushed the door open trying to grab me. I must have blacked out. The next thing I knew, I was in my room again with an awful headache. But I seem to remember someone whispering in my ear, 'You will have a little headache tomorrow, Maria, but you will believe you only had a bad dream.'"

"You know, I do feel like I've been living in a dream lately. The last thing I remember is being in Afghanistan. I can't remember coming home on leave."

Maria thought about what Robert just said. She recalled a "story" her grandfather told her about his near-death experience in Vietnam. He said that was why he could see the fallen heroes. He had solved many cases with their help. *I thought that were just stories. Oh my dear, Jesus, could this be happening to Robert too? I'm not sure if*

I should tell him about my grandpop's experience. If Robert is hurt somewhere, this may traumatize him, she thought.

Now it was time for them to go into the hidden darkroom.

"Maria, where is this room? I only see the wooden beams and walls."

"Well, you would never guess where. When Grandmom showed it to me, I could not believe it because grandpop was so creative. Look up at the ceiling. Can you see anything?"

He looked up. "What do you mean? This is a one-story house."

"That is what you are supposed to think," Maria said.

Tobit was very talented in making things look different from how they appeared. The key Maria held was a skeleton key. The keyhole was cleverly camouflaged in the mural on the wall. It has been many years since this secret entrance was opened. The key was not a key to a door but a mechanism lowering the ceiling with a set of stairs leading to the darkroom.

"No one was up here, Robert. Hurry up before someone or something comes back again."

They both entered the darkroom and pulled the stairs back up.

The room did not have much in it.

He looked around and said to her, "Sarah must have something here she wanted us to find."

*****

Shea, accompanied by two other fallen angels arrived at the Wright estate. They would try their best to find Maria and Robert without being detected.

"I hear a rookie hero angel named Sam is around trying to protect his friend. Well, we will see about that!" he said.

As they roamed around the estate, they reached Sarah's secret house which just didn't seem a secret anymore.

*****

"Sam, Robert and Maria are on the verge of finding a major clue in their investigation," Gabriel said, letting know that he was ready to get a chance to prove how important he was in helping them solve this long unsolved mystery.

"I am not sure what this is about, Gabriel; Robert never mentioned anything about his family or his involvement with Sarah and Tobit."

Gabriel told him all about Sara and Tobit's untimely death and their role in solving many mysteries so the angels can keep things safe for this world until their final battle was ready.

"Here we are, Sam," said Gabriel.

Sam replied, "I don't see a sign of anyone being here. Michael said they would be here."

"Let's go in. They have to be here; I can feel their presence," Gabriel said. "I know Sarah has a hidden darkroom."

They entered the house but could not see Robert or Maria.

"Gabriel, what do we do when we find them?" Sam asked.

"We must shield them from the enemy," the archangel answered.

"How can Maria see us? She hasn't crossed over yet."

"Sarah and Tobit shared their secrets with her because they knew that one day, she would take over their mission. When Maria was a little child, she was hit by a car and was bought back to life by the paramedics. She already saw some fallen angels, but she thought she was dreaming. And we have permission from on high to assist both Robert and Maria."

*****

"Hey, Maria, look at this. It's Sarah's old camera. I've never seen one like it. It looks old yet futuristic. Have you seen this before?" Robert wasn't real sure about how it even worked.

"Robert, this is what they want. But I don't know why I never saw my grandmom use this camera or whatever it is."

He replied, "If the camera was so important, why isn't it hidden in a better place?"

"Well, it is in her secret darkroom. But if someone was after them, Sarah probably tossed it up here and led her pursuers in a different direction."

Why is this so-called camera so important that Sarah and Tobit sacrificed themselves to protect it? That was what Maria and Robert now had to find out.

Sarah often told Maria stories of how God records our personal lives—both the good and not so good things that we have done—even though in His mercy we were forgiven of our faults. Somehow, the old memories we want to forget come up to bring us down.

This camera-like equipment needed to be put back up where it belonged: in the heavenly library of mankind. In the wrong hands, mankind can suffer emotional depression like never before. The guilt of their sins would be so embedded in their souls they would not hear the cries of God's mercy. That would be Satan's victory over the world.

"Maria, don't touch the camera. I think that is why I'm here. I have to bring it back to…" Robert hesitated.

Maria was confused. "Where do you have to bring it? What are you saying? We just found it. We don't even know what it does."

"I don't know. I don't even know how I got here, or if I'm really here at all. The last thing I remember is my good friend Sam dying in my arms, and then I passed out or got knocked out."

Chapter 3

Flashback of an Unwelcome Memory

"Sam, they're in the house," Gabriel said.

"Where? There is no one here, Gabriel."

"You will have to hold my hand. I will bring you to where they are."

Sam grabbed his hand, and they both transported to the second floor.

"They cannot see us yet," said Gabriel to Sam.

He began to tell him of his mission to help Maria bring back the device to where it belongs. Soon, Robert will be leaving her, and Sam will have to protect her from the ancient fallen ones.

*****

Maria picked up the device. When she did, she felt ashamed; and something in her told her how useless and unworthy she was to be alive.

Robert turned and saw her holding the box to her chest and weeping bitterly.

"Maria, let go of the camera!" Robert shouted.

"No! My grandparents deserve more than having me as their granddaughter! You don't understand. How can I continue their work when I'm not worthy?"

She was not acting at all like herself. She needed to let go or her life would be destroyed.

She felt herself going back to her upper teen years. It was a rebellious time in her life—for her and almost everyone else; that part when you knew about life before you even got started. There she was at a party that could have changed her life for the worst. Thank God she had good parents who cared to get involved. Knowing her parents wouldn't have let her go, she decided to go anyway. She let them believe she was staying over at a friend's house which her parents knew to be safe. And of course, that friend told her parents the same story.

Cynthia was Maria's best friend at the time. She picked up Maria from her house, and they headed up to the house of Cynthia's college boyfriend, Jeff, whom her parents knew nothing about. She just wanted to use Maria so she could have an excuse to see Jeff without her parents finding out.

There were other older boys and girls at the party along with a lot of alcohol and drugs. Maria never took drugs. Cynthia did, and she kept it to herself, but Maria soon found out the truth.

"Hey, Maria, I want you to meet someone. He is a friend of Jeff. This is Todd, Maria." Cynthia then went with Jeff up to his bedroom and left her alone with a perfect stranger.

"Oh...hi, Todd. Do you go to school with Jeff?"

He wasn't interested in small talk. He had a drink in his hand and was ready to give it to her.

Her cell phone went off; it was her mom. She couldn't answer the call because she knew her mom would hear the loud music, and she would know Maria wasn't where she said she was.

Todd put the drink in her hand and told her it was only soda. Then he asked her to go with him up to another bedroom where it would be quiet.

She did go with him, and she took the drink. After drinking it, she felt dizzy.

Todd began to take her clothes off. She did not know how long she was with him. But whatever he gave her made her have feelings she had never experienced before. She was feeling strong sexual urges that she could not control, and she was willing to go all the way to reach her desires.

Afterward, she heard her phone ring again. She pushed off who she thought was Todd. "I have to take this call; I'll be back. I'll take it in the bathroom so she can't hear us."

Maria was getting scared, and she knew she needed help, even if it was her mom and she would be in trouble too.

She locked the bathroom door. She was not sure if she could even talk to her mom because the drug Todd put in her drink was making her feel very incoherent.

She answered the phone, saying, "Help, Mommy." She tried to tell her mom where she was and blacked out.

Cynthia was with Jeff, getting high and letting him have his way with her.

Todd heard Maria talking to her mom and banged on Jeff's door. "Hey, guys, Maria locked herself in the bathroom. I think she told her mom to come get her."

"Let me get her out of here before her mom and dad get her. Jeff, just tell them we left for my house." Cynthia pushed open the bathroom door and tried to pick Maria up.

Jeff picked her up and put her in Cynthia's car.

Maria regained consciousness and saw Cynthia, who she thought was her friend, driving them away. "What are you doing? Why didn't you tell me what kind of party this was? Todd put something in my drink and had sex with me. I was so out of it. I'm not sure what happened. I thought you were my friend."

Cynthia began to cry. "I am sorry, Maria. I did not know he would do that. I wanted to tell you about Jeff, but I was afraid you wouldn't understand. I got mixed up with drugs. Jeff told me if I loved him, I would have sex with him. But I was afraid at first, then he told me to try the drugs, and I would feel so good having sex with him. It started with a drink he gave me, and I felt wonderful and free. Then we started to do more drugs. I tried to stop, and I couldn't. I'm sorry I got you into this; I needed a fix. I shouldn't have listened to him."

Maria said, "Go back to his house. My parents will be there. We will face it together, and they will help you."

Cynthia turned back. When she arrived at Jeff's house, both their parents were there with the police.

Cynthia turned to Maria and said, "I can't. My parents will be ashamed of me." She pushed Maria out of the car and sped off.

After her car turned off the road, there was an explosion. Cynthia went through a stop sign and toward oncoming traffic.

*****

"Sam, grab Maria now! And I will take the box from her!" Gabriel quickly grabbed the box, and Maria was unconscious but safe in Sam's arms.

"My dear, Jesus, what is happening?" Robert cried out. He could see Sam and Gabriel in the room. Then he became confused. "Sam! You're okay! I thought you died!"

"Robert, we will explain in a little while. Maria is gaining consciousness. She has something to share with you, and you will have to tell her what you've been holding back all these years."

Gabriel was letting him know that they had to be honest with each other before they finish their mission.

"Sam, we must give them privacy for a short time before you and Maria return the box."

Sam and Gabriel then turned away just for a moment.

*****

Maria began to awaken from her bad dream. She knew she had to tell Robert about what happened when she touched the device and confess to him what she had done and how guilty she felt because she could not help Cynthia.

"Robert, I am so ashamed of myself. There is more to tell you about that night and my mistake."

She began to finish what her vision from the box didn't show because Gabriel stopped her…

*****

Maria's parents took her from Jeff's house to the hospital. The doctor confirmed that Maria was raped. That was devastating to her parents and more so for Maria. She started to remember some of it; she thought there was someone else besides Todd. After Todd took her clothes off and started molesting her, someone else came into the room, but it sounded like a girl who was with a younger teenage boy.

Robert held Maria and began to remember something in his past as well. He knew he had to confess to her, just like Gabriel told him to do.

"Oh, Maria, I am sorry."

*****

That same day, Robert saw Cynthia at the store.

"Hey, Robby," Cynthia always called him that, "you coming to the party tonight? Your friend Maria will be there."

"What party? You mean the one near the college? I heard about it, but I can't believe Maria would go!" He replied.

"Well, I'm picking her up so her parents will think she's at my house."

"I'm surprised she would even be there. I'll go with my friend Sal. He asked me earlier, but I wasn't going to go. Since Maria is going, I'll go. Don't tell her, okay?"

He went home and gave his parents the same excuse, and his friend picked him up that night.

When they got there, Sal told Robert he had to see Jeff for something, and he would be right back. A young college girl started a conversation with him and began flirting with him.

"What's your name? You're really cute. You study here?" She knew he was too young to go to college, but she liked having young teens get excited about her.

Robert like the attention and fell for her hook, line, and sinker.

"You do drugs, Rob?"

"No, I don't. Do you?"

"Well, a little weed sometimes and, of course, a few beers to follow up." She held his hand and took him with her into an empty room. They sat on the sofa, and she began to kiss him. He started to move away. She told him to wait in the room so she can get him a drink. He told her not to give him an alcoholic drink; a soda will be good.

She didn't get him a soda; she gave him a beer.

"Here, you're in college now. Have just one beer." She convinced him, but she put something in the beer to make him relax for what she had in mind for him next.

Not knowing what to say, he took the beer; he didn't want her to know he was only sixteen. Halfway through his beer, he was all over the girl.

She made the first move; he made sure he would finish it. She led him up to one of the bedrooms. She then saw Todd in one of the rooms with a young girl. Turning to Robert, she told him to finish his beer. This way, the drug she gave him would fully get into his system. She wanted to be with Todd instead, so he brought Robert into the room with the college girl and decided to switch partners.

She took off Robert's clothes and led him to Maria. Maria and Robert were both high on the ecstasy drug that was in their drinks. Robert couldn't control his desires and was aggressive with Maria to reach his climax in the same way Maria experienced. Then Todd and his girlfriend went off to another room.

*****

After hearing Maria's story, he realized it was her he was with that night and not the strange girl at the party. He did confess to Maria not only for being at the party but also for what he had done to her.

She was upset at first and couldn't believe what she was hearing. Then she realized they were both victims. But Maria had more to tell him, something she did remember.

Just when she was about to tell him, the room filled with what looked like a wind tunnel. She went to hold on to Robert, but he vanished in front of her eyes.

"What is happening? Robert!"

But he was gone, and Maria was alone.

At least, she thought she was. Gabriel appeared to Maria first. She was frightened but not for long; she felt at peace as she looked at him.

"Are you an angel? Like the ones my grandfather told me about. I thought they were all just stories you told children at bedtime."

"Yes, I am. My name is Gabriel, and those stories Tobit told you were true. We have had many missions together. Our last mission was very challenging, to say the least. I will tell you all about them later. Now, I have someone I want you to meet."

Sam appeared in front of her.

"Maria, this is Sam. He is Robert's good buddy in the Marines who died in Afghanistan. He is now working with us. He is an unsung hero and on his first mission."

"And what about Robert? Is he dead too?" Maria could barely say the words that she hoped weren't true.

Gabriel gently told Maria that Robert was not dead, but he was in a coma at the veterans hospital.

She was relieved to hear that but could not hide her feelings of confusion and disbelief at what was happening to her. She thought she would never get a chance to finish her confession to Robert. But now wasn't the time to dwell about her past. She had to find out what this box had to do with her grandparents' death and where they had to take it.

Maria asked Gabriel what happened to the box. Gabriel could touch it because of his holiness and allegiance to the Creator. Sarah had it in a special case, but somehow, in her attempt to hide it in the darkroom, it opened, and she did not have time to put it back. Gabriel happened to retrieve the case after Sarah tried to get away.

Chapter 4

Conscious of the Mission Ahead

Robert was being pulled into the veterans hospital in Quantico. He kept saying Maria's name over and over, but he could not hear himself saying it. Finally reaching his destination, he could see a young man lying in a hospital bed. Outside the door, he could see an angel. He recognized him; it was Michael who saved him from the demon at Sarah's secret hideaway.

Michael entered the room and looked up. Seeing Robert, he held out his arms to guide him.

"Michael, who is that serviceman? Why am I here?" he asked. He then took a good look at the patient and realized that the Marine lying there was himself. "Michael, help me. Maria needs me!"

"It's okay, Robert. She is in good hands. And you will see her shortly because it is here where she must return the box. It is not a camera like you think. Instead of pictures, it stores memories that should not get into the wrong hands," replied Michael.

He then led him carefully down back into his body.

His vital signs were displayed in the nurses' station.

Nurse Pam quickly ran to his room. "Dr. Pompeii, please come to the emergency room number 126! Marine McDaniel is coming out of his coma."

Pam had been taking care of Robert since he came to the hospital a few weeks ago. She had been praying for him and was thanking God for having him come out of his coma.

"Thank you, sweet Jesus, for bringing this young Marine back."

After Pam had whispered her thanks, Robert opened his eye and called out Maria's name.

"Maria, Maria, don't let go!" He was holding on to Pam's hand.

Then he started to remember Michael leading him back to his body.

"It's okay, Robert. You are at the veterans' hospital, safe and sound. Your parents will be happy to hear that you are out of your coma," Pam said.

*****

His parents were on vacation in Ireland, and they just received the news about their son a few days ago. James and Rose McDaniel were devastated when they heard of their only son Robert being in a coma after a bomb struck him and five other Marines in Afghanistan. They knew about Sam as well because Robert wrote about him to them. They also met him once when they had leave time together. Sam did not have a family, and the McDaniels welcomed him as their own child. He also sent them letters. In Sam's last letter, he wrote about how he appreciated their hospitality and how proud they should be for having such a brave Marine for their son.

They did not know about Sam's death yet. They knew he was with their platoon, but they did not know he was one of the fatalities.

"We have to get home. Why is it taking so long to get a flight home? We should have been by his side when he was first brought home. I will never forgive myself for not being there for him," Rose said.

Her husband replied, "My dear, Rose, don't feel that way. We are in this together. We had no way of knowing what was going to happen. Trusting in God is all we can do. We have a flight first thing in the morning. We will have our luggage sent to the nearest hotel, and we will go straight to the hospital when we get back to the states."

James and Rose said a prayer together, and they felt a peace come over them.

Dr. David Pompeii came into the room, excited to see Robert awake.

"Young Marine, it is a miracle that you have come out of your coma. Do you remember anything that happened to you?" he asked.

"All I remember is holding on to my friend Sam. Then I found myself home again."

Robert stopped himself from telling him about seeing Maria. He knew no one would believe him. He would most likely tell Robert it was a dream. But in the room was someone who would believe it wasn't a dream looking across the room. Robert could see Pam, the nurse, smiling at him while the doctor was examining him. He wondered why he was not saying anything to her.

"You rest, young one. I will go ask one of the nurses to get you something to eat," the doctor said.

Robert thought, *Why don't you just ask Pam instead of calling someone else?* Then he realized she was more than his nurse; she was an unsung hero.

What was her journey to becoming a part of an elite group of angels serving under the archangels of the Lord?

*****

Pamela Wellington, a young nurse living in England during World War II, was inspired by the stories of a World War I nurse named Edith Cavell. She was in charge of a hospital for nursing in Belgium which was occupied by Germany during World War I. She took care of the wounded from both the Germans and the allies. Edith joined a Belgium underground movement to help many soldiers escape to neutral territories. Her bravery saved many soldiers. She was arrested and accused of treason and sentenced to execution.

Pam was inspired and wanted to try and take after her hero. She became a nurse at the young age of twenty-one. Pam helped take care of many people in England who had nowhere to go because of the devastating bombings by the Germans in World War II. She took care of mostly young children who were orphaned by the war.

One day, she saved an infant in the middle of the road. Once the child was safe, she went back to take care of the others, but she did not make it back. There was another bomb attack in the area; she was thrown across the road and then fell, hitting her head and blacking out. She came to and looked around, but everything was quiet; she could not hear a sound. Looking down, she saw herself lifeless and lying on a pile of rubble. Next to her was her guardian angel. He would lead her to her new destination.

*****

"Robert, I am here to help you and Maria. She and Sam must come here to this building and bring the box, but they have to do more than that. Her grandparents' souls are trapped in a portal, and they can't make the path over to heaven."

Pam started to tell Robert what the mission was for him and Maria but was interrupted by a very loud fire alarm. One of the patients, Harry Poindexter, set the alarm off at the end of the corridor. He was screaming that there were demons in his room planning to destroy the hospital by settling it aflame.

She had to leave Robert before telling him about their mission. She wanted to alert the heroes of what was happening and to make sure the archangels were keeping guard on Robert's room.

Pam noticed that a new angel was guarding Robert's door. She had never seen him before and wondered what had happened to Michael.

"What are you doing here? I don't remember seeing you before. And where is Michael?" she asked.

"My name is Az… I mean, Andy. Michael had an emergency back at the Wright estate. I happened to be here, and he told me to guard Robert."

It was Azza, the fallen one. He realized Pam would recognize his real name.

"Listen, Andy, or whoever you are. Michael wouldn't leave without letting me know where he was going. Now, who are you, and where is he?" She held her hand up to heaven and cried out for Michael to come to her aid.

Azza was a very strong fallen angel, but he was not stronger than Michael. He appeared to Pam in his true form to frighten her away. He was a massive creature.

"You can't stop us, Pam. We will stop both Maria and Robert from ever finding the portal and returning the box. Apollyon will cause all mankind to follow him. So don't bother Michael."

But Michael was not far behind him; he was fighting a demon trying to get to Harry Poindexter. Michael knew that Harry was just a curious bystander. After striking the demon spirit into the abyss before he could enter Harry, he turned and saw Azza ready to claim Pam for his trophy. Michael drew his sword and commanded Azza to leave, or he will be thrown into the abyss before his time.

"Now, go and tell Apollyon you have failed in your mission."

"Thank God you are here, Michael. I knew you would not put a new guardian here without telling me," Pam said.

Michael began to tell her about Harry, and that there wasn't any time to let her know he was leaving because it happened so quickly. Harry would have been a goner if he didn't come to his aid as fast as he did. Michael realized that was a diversion to get Robert out of the way. But Pam was very observant not to trust Azza.

Harry was a wanderer at the veterans' hospital. He has been there for at least six months. It so happened that he wandered off where he should have never been and saw what he shouldn't have seen; he actually found the part of the hospital that no one knew existed.

Harry quietly left his room by the nurses' station and was undetected. He could see someone or something waving for him to follow, and follow he did. There was a staircase, and painted on the door were NO EXIT and DO NOT ENTER. But Harry was too compelled to ignore the warnings and enter anyway.

Once he entered the staircase, he could not be seen by anyone else. When he looked back at where he came from, the door vanished. Harry began his journey down the staircase that seemed like it had no end. Finally, he reached the bottom. He thought he heard multiple voices crying out for help. Harry began to have a flashback from Vietnam: he heard the cries of his comrades burning alive in a village that the North Vietnamese razed to the ground. He tried to save them, but the fire was so intense; he had no choice but to leave with the rescue helicopter.

He started back up the stairway because he was being chased by a demon, called Belia, charged with bringing about weakness and guilt. He knew about Harry's weak spot and tried to make him feel guilty for leaving his friends to die. That was how he lured innocent souls. Harry's guardian angel was trying to lead him back to his room. When he finally got all the way up the staircase, he found the entrance back to his floor. Michael could hear his soul crying for help. Harry then hit the fire alarm. Michael put his wings around Harry to protect his soul.

Michael calmed Pam down and told her he was sending for Alexander to watch over Robert until Maria got there.

*****

"Gabriel, why is this box so important? Can't you just destroy it now?" Sam asked.

"Sam, you've seen what it did to Maria. She felt like her life was not worth living because of her guilt. If I weren't here, she would have gone on the path of no return, and the demon Belia would have captured her soul. And if Beelzebul gets hold of it, mankind will suffer a great loss of innocent souls. It is time to fill Maria in on why this is so important.

Chapter 5

THE TRUTH ABOUT THAT FATAL NIGHT

Maria began to cry bitterly. She always thought she could handle anything that came her way, especially since she was a Marine. She did not expect that this investigation would be such a spiritual epiphany that was as real as real could be.

Gabriel knew he had to tell Maria what happened that night eight years ago. But he had to do a condensed version because there was an urgency to get this mission completed.

He calmed her down and began to tell her of Sarah and Tobit's final mission. He began to tell Maria that Sarah wanted to let her know that her grandfather was telling her real stories, not fictional ones. They knew that, somehow, this would be their last mission. Sarah just wanted to retire and go back to Maine and try to have a peaceful retirement, but she knew that would never happen. This was one mission that had to get done, or there would be nothing to retire for and that Tobit sometimes wished he never even started with the special forces and kept Sarah safe.

Not far from the Quantico veterans' hospital, there was a burst of light in the sky, then there was an explosion. Tobit was told to go and investigate the incident. He had brought a small crew with him including the bomb squad. They could see from a distance an amber whirlwind, but it did not travel from place to place. It just hovered in one spot. When they finally arrived at the site, Tobit and the agents saw a handsome angel in the fiery flames, but only Tobit could sense pure evil.

The handsome angel, the only spiritual entity at the site, took a box and came toward him. He was just about to grab it when Raphael stood between the evil angel and Tobit, commanding him not to touch it. Raphael was able to touch it and take it away from the fallen angel. He gave Tobit orders to go back to the hospital, and Michael, the archangel, would give him instructions for him and Sarah to protect the box and keep it out of the hands of the most high fallen one. Raphael put the box in a special case, and the box vanished in his hands.

Tobit gave the agents the order to investigate the area and find out what caused this phenomenon. Then he went to the hospital to meet with Michael. He had no idea what this box was or where it had vanished to.

Tobit arrived at the hospital and had no idea where to meet Michael. He had an office at the hospital because he also counseled the young soldiers coming in from battles. He started for his office and saw a young gentleman waving at him to follow him. He led him to the end of the hospital and a door he had never seen before. After going through the door, he turned around and saw a wall instead of a door, and the one who led him there vanished. He looked around and noticed a stairway and began to descend through what seemed like a never-ending staircase. He heard a mixture of prayers and cries for help. Finally, he got to the end, and he was greeted by Michael.

Tobit questioned Michael and was bewildered at the fact that he did not know of this place. He had been working with Michael for many years. Michael told him there are places like this all across the globe and that Tobit was the first human being ever to be there. Michael didn't have time to go into the details, but he gave Tobit the case with the box in it and told him to go back to his estate and hide it until it was time to return it to the dimension where the enemy cannot expose it to this nation.

Michael then warned him not to open the box no matter what happens. He must put it in the center of the pond on his property. It would be guarded by Alexander and his team of fallen heroes.

Tobit took the box and went back to the house to do as Michael had told him. In the parking lot of the hospital, a group of fallen angels schemed to interfere with Tobit's plans and get the box back to their master. They swiftly flew to the estate before Tobit could get there.

*****

Meanwhile, back at the house, Sarah had an unexpected visit from her twin sister, Jean. She couldn't wait for Sarah and Tobit to retire in Maine with her. The siblings were very close while growing up. They often traded places with each other to fool their friends, but their parents would catch on very quickly. Of course, they discouraged that behavior. Sarah was so happy to see her that she dropped what was in her hands and ran to meet her.

Tobit tried to call ahead to let Sarah know what was happening, but there was no answer. While driving to his destination, it began to rain. The wind picked up, and it was hard for Tobit to see where he was going. This was an opportunity for one of the fallen, Azza, to try and cause an accident so he could retrieve the box and return it to his master. Azza quickly went ahead and pushed down a huge tree to block Tobit's path. As the tree was about to crash down, two of Alexander's companies of fallen heroes tossed it in another direction.

*****

Back at the estate, not only did Jean surprise Sarah but also her daughter Gloria stopped by with her daughter Maria. She wanted Sarah to watch Maria for the weekend while she and her husband Joseph went to visit their friend. Sarah did not have a clue that she too was going to be busy, but she loved having Maria around to visit.

There was going to be a battle that night between the angels to save mankind—a battle that would become deadly for two human heroes. Alexander and his company guided Tobit safely to his estate. But when he arrived, he didn't count on having guests. He rushed in to see Sarah to explain their new mission. Sarah could see in his face that something was wrong.

Maria stopped Gabriel from continuing his story because she remembered something from that night.

"Gabriel, I remember seeing the box. When Grandpop rushed into the house, I was so happy to see him, and I thought he had a present for me. But when I went to go near him to give him a hug, he looked upset about something. He turned and put the box on top of the china cabinet then gave me a big hug and kiss. He told me how much he missed me, but he and Grandmom had to be alone for a minute to talk. I then went with Jean to the other room. I don't know how I forgot about that."

Gabriel reminded Maria that she experienced a great trauma that night. He asked her if she remembered what happened when Jean left the room. She was puzzled as to why he asked that question. She started to remember that it wasn't her grandparents who brought her over to Robert's parents' house; it was Jean. How did she come up with that other recollection?

Jean was a good person, but she innocently got involved in supernatural activity, which she had little knowledge of the consequence. She just got mixed up the wrong friends. It started in her college years with meditations. During some of her meditations, what she thought was an Angel of God was just the opposite. Sarah had serious talks with her about how dabbling in what she was doing will have severe consequences; Jean assured Sarah she was just trying to relax because it had been so stressful at school. Jean did not tell Sarah of her experience during her mediation and never practiced it again. But the angel she summoned was not going to let her go that easily.

Jean came into the dining room where Tobit and Sarah were trying to figure out what to do about the mission.

"Hey, I thought you guys needed time to talk, so I sent Maria to Robert's parents' house for the night. Was that okay? I am just going to the guest room. You two are always so secretive."

For once, Jean just wanted to be involved in their secret life.

Tobit anxiously looked at Sarah then went to look up at the china cabinet. But the box was missing.

"Oh, Lord! What happened to the box?"

Sarah didn't see him with it when he came in, so she questioned him to try and understand why this box was so important. Sarah told Tobit that her sister was near the cabinet when she was in the room.

Tobit started to rush to the guest room. Suddenly, in the corner of his eye, he saw a small legion of fallen angels on the side porch. Sarah told Tobit to get in touch with Michael or Alexander while she figured out what Jean was doing with the box. Tobit grabbed Sarah and kissed her tenderly, told her to be careful, and that he loved her so much.

"*Jean*! Are you in your room?" Sarah was horrified to think that something would happen to her sister.

"I am okay, Sarah. I am sorry. I was going to look in the box, but I realized it was not mine to look at. I could almost hear someone telling me to get the box and bring it out to the backyard. She sounds like..." Jean was frightened to tell Sarah of the angel she summoned years ago. Then she began to scream in horror. "Look out! There she is! She's trying to take the box from us!"

"Who is it? I can't see her. Is she nearer to you or me?" Sarah was trying to get a straight answer, but Jean was so frightened and couldn't believe what was happening. "Jean, give me the box and look at me. We are going down the stairs and ask Tobit what to do with this."

They made it to the staircase, but there was an angel named Bella in the middle of the stairs ready to nudge Sarah's hands so she can release the box. Sarah began to lose her balance and she let go of Jean. The box flew out of their hands and down the stairs. Bella pushed Jean and Sarah down the stairs and went after the box.

Tobit had a special firearm made just for battles with the fallen angels. It was an amber laser which, when aimed at the lost souls, banished them to their eternal punishment. The legends on the pouch meant the battle was just beginning.

Alexander and his fallen heroes were ready to help Tobit to make this mission possible. The fallen demonic angels were on the verge of defeat. Tobit heard shouting from the house and ran over to see what was going on. Jean was running out, looking for Bella, with Sarah following her. Sarah then ran to Tobit to find out once and for all what they were supposed to do with the box; Tobit told Sarah they had to drop the box in the middle of the lake and leave it until it was time to retrieve it. She told Tobit a soul-catcher named Bella stole the box to give to her master.

Jean heard what they were saying. She summoned Bella and told her she could have her soul completely if she returned the box. And Bella yearned for Jean's soul for years and needed that sensuous feeling of having a woman's soul. These soul-catchers felt an extreme ecstasy between them and their soul-givers. Jean had part of that experience and knew that Bella could not resist.

Bella handed the box to Sarah and quickly embraced Jean telling her to relax because this would be the best feeling she would ever have in her human experience. Bella knew she had to be alone with Jean, so she headed back to the house and into the guest room. Jean was ready to protect her sister, and she felt this mission was very important to not only Sarah and Tobit but for our country. She knew she had to meditate so that Bella could finally possess her soul.

Bella laid Jean down on the bed to begin her meditation chant. Jean's heart slowed down, and Bella's excitement slowly started to arouse her.

Sarah told Tobit to bring the box to the boat. She was not going to let Jean give her soul to the dark side. Tobit agreed and started for the lake with Alexander by his side. Sarah was accompanied by Pamela, the angel from the hospital who often worked with Sarah on other mission, and headed for the guest room. They also needed more help from Raphael to destroy Bella for good. Raphael let Sarah know they had to work very quickly because once Bella gets Jean's soul, there was no way to get it back.

They all entered the room just as Jean's soul was ready to unite with Bella. Sarah reached for Jean to wake her from her trance. Pamela called out to Bella to back off. Finally, Raphael caught Bella in her vulnerable state of ecstasy and sent her to her final eternal punishment. Then he touched Jean and returned her entire soul back where it belonged.

Sarah turned to Jean and asked her to continue the mission with her. They proceeded to the lake. Catching up to Tobit, they headed for the boat. Now that Bella was gone and most of the demons were vaporized, they almost accomplished what Tobit came to do.

Sarah assured Tobit that Jean was fine, and that Raphael restored her soul. Tobit noticed Alexander was having more evil ones coming in for the kill. Michael was needed quickly, and Pamela was on her way to get him.

Just before they could get to the boat, a bolt of lightning struck their path. The enemy was determined to stop them. Tobit told the girls to take the other route to the boat while he acted as a decoy to keep the demons from following them. And it worked; Tobit had the box.

Sarah and Jean finally reached the boat. One sister made it near the boat and took the box from Tobit so he could guide them toward the boat. The other sister was not far behind. Tobit was a few feet from the boat and did not realize how close he was because of the smoke from the lighting strike. Then came another strike and, this time, it hit the boat. The box flew out of one of the sister's hands and onto land. No one knew what had happened. But someone did spot it, and she knew it was too late to get back into the boat because it was destroyed along with its passengers.

Michael finally arrived, but it was too late for Tobit and one of the sisters. It was not Sarah but Jean who was in the boat. Sarah ran to her secret house on her estate to her darkroom and put the box up there. She went back to the house and realized the enemy would be looking for her and not Jean.

Michael and Alexander finished the fight. As far as the demons knew, the box was in a safe place that they could not reach, at least for now. Michael knew who Sarah was. He told her to take her sister's identity. When the authorities arrived, they confirmed it was an act of nature. Sarah lost her husband and sister and was devastated. How could she keep this heartbreaking experience from her loved ones?

Gabriel had to let Maria know the whole story. He knew Maria was strong enough to handle the truth. The future of the nation was now in Maria's and Robert's hands.

This news about her grandmom being alive was very shocking to Maria. She loved her so much, and when she thought of the terrifying nightmare of that night, she was angry and joyful at the same time. Gabriel comforted her but let her know how crucial it was for Sarah to conceal her identity.

Maria asked Gabriel how the fallen angels knew where to go when her grandpop brought the box to their estate. He said that some of the agents are into satanic practices. They may have been some of Tobit's friends. There were many parties in our country working with these occult groups trying to destroy our economy and taking freedom away from people so that the Antichrist would come and pretend to help them by having the government take control of their lives. They knew that if they got their hands on this box, people would give up hope in themselves.

Maria realized that she and Robert had to find out where the leak in the agency came from. These people were responsible for the deaths of her grandpop and great-aunt.

Chapter 6

TESTED BY FIRE

"It's time to go and see Robert. You will both be present to witness the freedom of the souls beneath the hospital. The Archangel Raphael will take the box and capture all their guilt that keeps them from entering paradise," said Gabriel.

He then assured Maria that her mission would not be in vain.

Maria asked Gabriel, "How can we get there in time? My parents will be home soon, and the hospital is about an hour away! What happened to Sam? He was just here with us!"

Gabriel reminded her that there is nothing impossible for God and that Sam was transported to see Robert before they arrived there. He assured Maria that Sam would be okay. Spreading his wings around Maria, they both vanished from the estate.

In the blink of an eye, Maria and Gabriel were outside the hospital. Then Gabriel vanished, and it was Michael who was with her.

"Maria, I will go in with you to see Robert. But remember, only you can see me."

"What happened to Gabriel?" she asked.

Michael told her that Gabriel was the messenger tasked with telling her what happened and what's about to happen. But now Michael will prepare her for her mission with Robert and Sam.

Maria walked into the hospital. They came in after visiting hours, but she showed her Marine's ID and explained that a young

Marine just got up from a coma, and he wanted her by his side. The receptionist was sympathetic and told her which room Robert was in.

Sam was by Robert's bedside. He still wasn't sure of what he was there to do or why, but Gabriel told him he will play a major role in the lives of Robert and Maria.

Robert was awakened when Sam touched his shoulder. He was able to see Sam, and he started to cry because of what happened back in Afghanistan.

"I am so sorry you didn't make it back with me. But I am more joyful that God has given me the vision of your spiritual form. I don't understand what is happening with Maria and me, but knowing that you are helping and taking care of us gives me peace of mind." Robert also let Sam know how much he meant to him and his family.

Michael appeared in the room to let them know Maria was coming too.

Robert said to Michael, "I am feeling weak from not moving. How can we all get to the souls to set them free?"

Raphael, the archangel for healing, appeared in the room. Immediately, he and Michael laid their hands on Robert. Robert then sat up and regained his strength.

Maria walked into the room, and her eyes immediately focused on Robert.

She ran to him, put her arms around him, and gave him a kiss. "It's really you in person! I still can't believe all this is happening to us," she said.

For a brief moment, the vision of an angelic dimension was not visible to either of them.

Robert embraced Maria as well and tenderly kissed her back. "This isn't a dream, is it? We wanted to find out what happened to your grandparents, and it turned into a whole life-changing experience. We don't even know what happened to them yet, and now we have a mission from God to *save souls* and our country. I still can't comprehend it all, but I know we have to be committed to this for ourselves."

"Robert, this isn't a dream," Maria said. "I have so much more to tell you. I did find out what happened to my grandparents. It's a long story, but I will tell you after we do what the archangels told us to do. And Robert, I love you."

He held Maria in his arms and kissed her and whispered in her ear, "I love you too."

As they embraced, Michael appeared. "My children, it's time to move on and free some souls."

Then they were able to see Gabriel and Sam.

They still had many questions for Michael and Gabriel about what was to come. The biggest question was, how do they leave the room without being stopped by the nurses?

Michael knew he had to be with them on this mission. He let them know that there would be a diversion of incoming wounded soldiers and Marines from Afghanistan. The nurses would be too busy to notice them leaving. And Michael and Gabriel would cloak them with their wings, which would make them invisible to the staff.

There was a small army of fallen angels and demon followers ready to stop what was about to happen. They did not want to lose without a fight. Maria and Robert looked out the door and noticed a few demons lurking in the corridor.

"Michael, I'm getting frightened. We need you to pray for us before we begin. Why do we have to do this? We are only human. What power do we have to defeat these creatures?" Maria asked.

Michael replied, "I will give you both a blessing before we leave this room. God gave His disciples the power and tested them many times. They proved to Jesus they were worthy by their perseverance, and He gave them the Holy Spirit which took their fears away and gave them the strength to finish their missions."

He then laid hands on both of them and recited a scripture from John 10:27–30: "My sheep hear my voice, and I know them and they follow me; and I give them eternal life, and they shall never perish, and no one will snatch them out of my hands. My Father, who has given them to me, is the greatest of all, and no one is able to snatch them out of the Father's hand. I and the Father are one.

"Bless your children of the most Holy Father. They need your Spirit now to go and complete their mission to bring your eager souls to their final resting place in your kingdom; in Jesus, your son's name, Amen."

Maria and Robert felt the power of God come upon them. They both gave thanks and were ready to go into battle with their comrades to do the will of God.

Before they left the room, Michael summoned extra angels to clear the path for Maria and Robert. Closing his eyes, he mentally called on Alexander and his troops. He also called on two saints: Nereus and Achilleus—Roman soldiers who were martyred for converting to Christianity in the fifth century. The two gave up the swords of the Roman Empire for new swords with blinding light to send the fallen ones to their eternal punishment.

Michael allowed Nereus and Achilleus to go in front of Maria and Robert, giving their swords the power to put down the evil demons lurking in the corridor. He then shadowed Maria and Robert with his wings. Gabriel and Sam were also close behind them.

As soon as the two former Roman soldiers stepped out into the corridor, demons tried to frighten them off. But the courageous soldiers of Christ held up their bright golden swords which sent the demons screaming with horror to their destiny of eternal punishment.

But there was a stronger entity that can be destroyed only by the archangels. His name was Beelzebul. Achilleus knew of his strength and that their swords would not stop him so easily.

Nereus lift his sword and encouraged Achilleus to do the same. Then he shouted, "In the name of the Most High Jesus Christ and with our companions the archangels behind us, we command you to go from which you came until your time for eternal punishment is due!"

Beelzebul knew he could not win, but he had to distract these guards to weaken the two mortals and stop them from taking back the poor souls trapped in the hospital's lower floor. He mentally summoned his fallen followers to get behind Sam and Gabriel and somehow distract them. What could they possibly do that would distract them from their mission? Gabriel had the box, and Sam had his eyes on Maria and Robert.

*****

Five hours earlier, Sarah (who was back in Saint Albans, Maine) had a dream about what happened eight years ago that made her feel as though it was happening all over again. But in this dream, she was just watching the whole nightmare happening before her eyes and in panoramic view. When she looked to the side, she could see Gabriel talking to a young woman and showing her the sequence of events as they happened. She said to herself, *She looks just like my little Maria.*

She took her eyes away for a second, and she witnessed what she didn't see before: Jean, ready to give Bella her soul just to get the box. She was there when Bella was trying to get Jean's soul. She realized why Bella was more interested in her pleasure with Jean than getting the box to her former demon friends. Thank God Raphael saved her in time. If Bella has completed her own mission, Jean would have been just like Bella, waiting for her next victim.

Then she looked and saw herself and Jean running toward the boat. Again, her eyes focused on the woman, but this time, she knew it was Maria.

She began to yell at Gabriel, "No! Don't let her see what really happened!"

Gabriel looked at Sarah and told her it was time.

She returned to her vision of all that unfolded that horrifying evening. Her beloved husband and her sister, who almost gave her soul to help her and Tobit, went up in flames. She began to weep bitterly, wondering why this had to happen.

Sarah awoke from her dream and shook with fear. She told herself it was only a dream, but she knew that it had to be more. She prayed to God for guidance on what this vision meant; was it real or just a bad nightmare? She's had many dreams since the incident, but none of them were as real as this one was. Did God want her back on the force? And why couldn't she see the angels anymore, especially Tobit and Jean?

Suddenly, Pamela appeared to her. She told her she was needed again and that only Maria knew her true identity.

"Pamela, what happened to Tobit and Jean? Why aren't they helping us?" Sarah asked.

Pam replied, "Jean's soul had to be purged and was going to purgatory, but Tobit was pleading on her behalf. In the midst of the battle going on around them, both their souls were swept away by Beelzebul and trapped with the others beneath the hospital."

"How can this be? He has no power over us!" Sarah said.

She knew that God was always there for us, but being human, we always questioned what we didn't understand, especially when it came to our families.

Pamela took Sarah's hand and began to pray with her. "Father in heaven, bring down your Spirit upon us so we may get through this trial with the knowledge that doing your will is for your glory and for the good of your people. We know you can save these souls without us, but you love us so much you include us in your works to lead others to your heavenly kingdom. Amen."

Sarah began to cry because she felt unworthy for doubting the Lord; at the same time, she wept for joy because after hearing Pamela's prayer, she was proud that God had chosen her and her granddaughter to help do His will.

"I am ready to do whatever it is to release the souls to their journey with Jesus. I understand now what we have to do and why. Pamela, thank you for giving me courage and bringing me to my senses." She felt like she could not thank her enough.

Sarah had packed her bags and was headed for the airport. This would be a surprise visit from Jean—yes, she had to keep up the charade of being Jean. She could have been sent there faster with the guidance of an angle, but she and Pamela had to make it convincing for the family. Taking a plane would be much faster than driving.

Pamela had filled her in on what was going on at the estate, so she knew that Gloria and Joseph would not be there until tomorrow afternoon. She also had a key to let herself into her own house.

It took Sarah about two hours altogether to get to the estate. Once she unpacked, she waited awhile to hear what it was that she had to do. Pamela began to tell her about Robert being involved in this mission. She also told Sarah of the danger the contents of the box could have on mankind.

Pamela told her about what Maria experienced when she touched the camera-like object without the protective case. Sarah was not aware of Maria having teenage problems, and she regretted not being there for her granddaughter when she needed her most. Being silent for all these years was a tremendous sacrifice, but it was one she knew she had to uphold. Being her aunt while incognito, she did see her graduate and was there for her after boot camp.

Maria's parents kept quiet about some personal things that the family did not want anyone to know. In fact, there was more to her story after the party which kept Maria from her "Aunt Jean" for about six months. Her parents told Jean she was in some boarding school, and that was why she could not come to visit her.

Now Sarah knew the whole story about Maria and Robert and where they were and what they must do with the help of Michael and Gabriel. And of course, who could forget Sam? He would be of great value to Robert and Maria.

Suddenly, the Archangel Raphael appeared to Sarah and Pamela. "Peace to you both. I have come to take you to a safe distance from the porthole where souls are. You will witness their souls being set free."

"Oh, Raphael. Will I see Tobit and Jean? I miss them so much."

Sarah just wanted to be reassured, especially for Jean.

"Many souls will be released, Sarah. And you can be assured we will see Tobit. He will still be needed for many missions to come. Jean will go to her place with Jesus because of her bravery."

Sarah asked Pamela and Raphael if she could have a moment alone just to get her thoughts together. They agreed but just for a short time; they were getting close to the release of souls. Sarah began to have flashbacks of her horrifying experience. She thought to herself, *It has been so long. I don't know if I can handle Tobit really being gone. I wish Tobit was here with me because I miss him being a part of my life.*

She began praying: "Dearest Jesus, the pain of being without Tobit was just subsiding. But now I have that heartbreaking feeling of losing him all over again. Give me your peace knowing that it will never be the same without him. Even though I may work with him on cases. I know that at the end of the day, he will not come home with me, and I will never be Sarah to my family; I will always be Jean even to my own daughter. Pray, dear Jesus, to your Heavenly Father for me, Sarah. Help me to do your will until I someday see you face to face. Amen."

Raphael and Pamela walked over to Sarah and felt her aching heart. Putting their arms around her, they also prayed for her and for the success of the mission ahead of them. Raphael quoted scripture from 1 Corinthians 10:13: "No trial has come to you but what is human. God is faithful and will not let you be tried beyond your strength; but with the trial he will also provide a way out, so that you may be able to bear it." Hearing this from Raphael gave Sarah the answer to her prayer.

*****

Azza managed to get behind Gabriel and Sam as instructed by Beelzebul. He was not alone; there were at least five others with him. He had a plan; he would try to recruit Sam to their side which would distract Gabriel into protecting Sam. Sam was young blood to the experienced demon, and he will be allowed to put him to the test.

Azza got close enough to whisper in his ear. "Do you remember just before you went to war? The few friends who had taken you out tried to get you drunk so you would meet up with someone at the hotel. The guys brought a young girl in after they got her to have a drink. Poor Lori, she was a virgin, wasn't she, Sam? They put something in her drink. They wanted you and the twenty-one-year-old to have sex. Her friends took her out for the same reason. It's a shame your buddies go so drunk; they couldn't wait for you."

Sam began to weep because he remembered that night and how they took advantage of that young girl Lori. When it was his turn to be with her, Sam told his friends he wanted to be alone with her since it was his first time. She was starting to come to and began crying. He had no intention of using her. He told her to call her parents and the police. She knew he was not at fault for what had happened. They went out the door, and he left the hotel and made sure she was safe. He felt ashamed and not worthy to be with Gabriel and to help his friends.

Gabriel didn't know Sam was being tormented with thoughts of guilt. Looking over his shoulder, Gabriel saw Azza ready to snatch Sam from his sight. He had to act quickly to save him.

He was ready to go with Azza. He could feel a warm feeling of pleasure just from Azza's touch which lasted for only a short time but was long enough for him to want to go to the dark side.

Gabriel then broke off the line to save Sam. That was when the demon forces had a chance to get to Robert.

Michael felt that something was not right. He had to concentrate on keeping Maria and Robert safe and get to their destination.

He began to speak to Maria. "We are having a weak link behind us. You must hold on to Robert. We must stick close together and keep prayer in your minds. Evil is trying to enter your thoughts. Gabriel is battling with Azza to save Sam."

Robert heard Michael and demanded to go back and help Sam. But Michael told him that Gabriel was more than capable of helping Sam. Even though Gabriel was outnumbered, other angels would be summoned to help.

The guardian angels of the fallen heroes were there to get Sam back before it was too late. Mathew, Sam's guardian angel, was alerted that he needed help, and he gathered all the other guardian angels to help. Mathew touched his shoulder and told him to let go of Azza's hand.

"Sam, I was there when you saved Lori. She is now working for God, helping young women have self-esteem and leading many to Jesus. You are worthy, Sam. If it wasn't for you, Lori would have died that night and been lost forever."

Gabriel drew his sword, and the bright light from his sword frightened the demons enough to withdraw. Azza drew his sword too, but Gabriel knew he had no power over him. So did Azza, but he did not want to face Beelzebul after failing his mission.

Sam was trying to let go of Azza. Mathew saw Sam trying to let go; he knew he could pull him off of Azza. Because Sam willed it, he was freed. Azza was then ready to face his eternal punishment in hell.

Michael informed Robert that Sam was safe. Gabriel told Sam he was now in charge of the guardian angels to protect the line that was broken.

They all followed Sam and chanted, "In Jesus's name, flee, demons in the rear!"

One by one, they turned into gray vapor that filled the corridor.

All but one, the spirit of doubt, broke the line of protection. Sam, still struggling with all the confusion around him, managed to see something over Robert's shoulder. But he was distracted because a few more evil spirits were trying to shield the guardian angels from getting to the one on Robert's shoulder. This spirit was undeserved guilt spirit trying to make you feel guilty about a situation you had no control over. There was a dark mist around Robert; it was a test allowed by Michael to strengthen Robert's faith.

*****

The spirit of doubt whispered in Robert's ear. "Do you really think what happened to Sam was not your fault? You know, he would not even have been there if you didn't insist that he should be with you on that mission. You said you can't remember what happened. Let me help you with a little flashback."

Suddenly, Robert was back in Afghanistan, just before the enemy's ambush. Sam came to report a suspicious group of Marines. They were in American uniforms, but they were keeping close together. Robert and Sam went to the commanding officer because Robert didn't want to make a decision on his own. They both didn't realize that time was not in their favor.

Sam told Robert he came to him because he couldn't find the commanding officer. He thought he saw him with the group of

Marines, but he disappeared behind the tanks. Sam knew Robert was next in command, and he would have to make that call.

"You went to look for the commanding officer. You should have listened to Sam and made that decision to go see who these strangers were. Just as you turned away, what happened, Robert? Sam saw the enemy raising their AK-47s, and he gave his life to save yours. You are responsible for your best friend's death."

*****

Maria felt Robert slumping onto her. The spirit of doubt was grinning at his attempt to undo what Raphael had done for Robert; doubt would cause him not to accept his healing. Maria yelled for Michael to help, but Michael knew that this time, it was Sam's mission to help his friend.

Sam knew what he had to do. He loved his friend as a brother. He felt to his knees and raised his hands to the heavens pleading with God to forgive him of anything that he has ever done in his life. "God, I am your servant now and forever. Whatever I need to do, let me know now."

Then it was as if time stood still; Sam looked around him. No one was moving, and bright light descended around him. He heard a voice coming from the light.

"You are forgiven, and you are chosen to be an instrument for God. I give you my Spirit of fire. You will have the strength to save Robert from the evil that is trying to possess him."

The flames of the Holy Spirit came upon Sam. He was lifted from his knees. His appearance appeared stronger; he was in full armor ready for battle. And he was given a sword to defend Robert against the guardian angel of doubt and guilt.

The brightness from Sam's sword filled the whole corridor. The evil spirit was blinded. Sam ordered him to flee, and the evil spirit crawled on its belly and begged for mercy. No mercy could be given, and he vanished without a trace.

Sam lowered his sword and pulled Robert to his feet. "You know better not to believe the lies of our enemy. You did your job of protecting your unit. The demon lied to you about what happened. You were the Marine who saw the enemy, and you saved your men by giving us a warning. Most of us were saved. I saved your life because God had other plans for me. And now, we will work together to fight the real evil in the world—one that can't be seen by humans. You are my brother now and always. Let us go into this battle victoriously."

Michael turned to Sam. "Well done, Sam. You are now ready to be the leader of the guardian angels. The Spirit of God is upon you. Blessed be to God."

Robert became strong again and asked Sam to lead the way. Sam was proud to give his life for his friend. In his new eternal life, he would be a courageous angel encouraging Robert whenever he needed him.

*****

Rose and James McDaniel were in a taxi on their way home. They could not get a hotel near the hospital because they were all fully booked. Then they realized they rented out their house for a month to vacationers.

Rose asked James, "Why don't we just go and see if anyone is at the Wright estate? Believe it or not, I still carry the key to their house. I'm sure we can let ourselves in just until morning. Then we can go and see Robert."

James replied, "Before we left for our trip, Joseph told me they were coming to the estate to try and sell it. Maybe we will get lucky, and they will be there."

Sarah left a note for Gloria and Joseph telling them she came for a surprise visit. Not seeing anyone home, she decided to visit a friend, and she would return in the morning. She signed the note, "Love always, Jean."

*****

Raphael let Sarah know that it was time. He spread his wings over Pam and Sarah; and in the blink of an eye, they were near the entry of the porthole of lost souls.

Just as they vanished, Rose and James's taxi pulled up to the house. James rang the doorbell, but no one answered. Rose pulled out her key, and they let themselves in.

After they put their luggage in the foyer, Rose called out to make sure no one was home. "Gloria, are you home?"

Getting no answer, both looked around the house hoping to see some evidence that the Thompsons were actually staying at the estate. There were some dishes in the sink, and going upstairs, they saw luggage in the bedroom. They also noticed some luggage in the second bedroom.

"I wonder who else came with them? I know Maria is in the service. Maybe she had some leave time. You think she knows about Robert?" James asked.

Rose looked in the room and noticed that Maria's uniform was hanging on a post.

"Yes, James. I think Maria did come with them. We should bring our things to the other bedroom. We should get some rest now because we will have a long day tomorrow, and I am so tired from our long flight."

Just before they went to bed, Rose noticed a letter on the table addressed to Gloria and Joseph.

"Look, James. It's a letter from Jean. She says she had to visit a friend about a personal matter, and she hopes they didn't mind that she let herself in. Oh, that night was so dreadful. Jean witnessed her own sister's death. She was a dear friend of ours. I miss her so much."

James tried to console Rose. "My dear, I miss them too. They are in the Lord's hands now. Let's go and get some rest. I am looking forward to seeing our son, and I am so grateful that he is alive. Thank you, Jesus, for sparing us from the grief of losing our son."

Rose embraced her husband, and they retired for the night.

Chapter 7

Can Old Friends Be Trusted?

There was something going on at the agency in a hidden room only known to a few. There were chanting people in black hooded robes conjuring the spirit of darkness. And this spirit would appear, surprising the congregation of loyal agents pretending to be American agents, just to bring our country to its knees. They began to lie facedown in worship of Beelzebul.

The leader of this group of Satan worshipers was a good friend of Tobit Wright. And Tobit went to his grave not knowing the truth about his friend's betrayal.

His name was Charles Booths. He and Tobit knew each other a long time. Charles didn't have many friends. He was an "A" student and vas very shy and had a hard time talking to others. His parents passed away when he was about twelve years old. His grandfather took him in, but his health was poor, so he usually stayed over at Tobit's house.

Then they went their separate ways: Tobit went to the Naval Academy, and Charles decided to go to Berkeley College where he had a full scholarship. But in their senior year of high school, Charles and Tobit promised to be buddies forever. They kept that promise. When Charles was a college freshman, he still kept in touch with

Tobit through letters, even on holidays. And whenever they came home, Charles was always welcome at the Wright's house.

Then they reached junior year in college; Tobit heard less from his friend. He was getting involved with a close group of friends. They called themselves "the small circle of friends." But that circle grew from a few hundred into a little more than a thousand. These so-called friends just preyed upon the lonely and students with low self-esteem.

Meditations were frequently used in the group. These meditations came from the Kundalini—a demonic spirit which is known as a counterfeit Holy Spirit. These were the same meditations Jean started to get into when she attended her college. Charles joined this group because they made him feel wanted. And while doing this practice, he was coming out of his shell.

Unlike Jean, who was eventually freed from her angel Bella, Charles took his meditations to its limits. It changed him from being a humble and gentle young man into a self-centered and aggressive one. He had started out innocently meditating to relax and trying to give himself more confidence. He was told that the spirit would give him all the confidence he would need to do whatever he desired. He felt uncomfortable doing mediations with groups of people, so he started meditating by himself, which was recommended to him by the founder of the small circle of friends, Martin Gomez, and his wife Sally.

He was not sure how to begin, and Sally was more than eager to show him. She came to his dormitory late at night to teach him the practice of Kundalini. After just a few weeks of meditating with Sally, he was ready to try it on his own. After about a month of doing it on his own, he felt like he needed more. The next step was having the spirit of strength and more confidence in himself.

Sally was hoping he would ask her for help. Charles was a very attractive young man but extremely shy with women. She wanted him to be more than a teacher. She was faithful to her husband, but she had received a dark angel from her trance in the demon spirit. She thought it was okay to share her angel with others, and that it wasn't cheating even though she could physically feel ecstasy. Finally, she persuaded Charles to join her and help him find his angel. He was hesitant at first but gave in because he wanted to build up his self-esteem.

Sally came to Charles's house, and he welcomed her in. She made herself comfortable by sitting on his floor with her yoga mat. He told her he had to get his mat, and he set it down facing Sally. She held his hands and told him to relax as they have practiced before.

For the first time, Charles could feel a presence he never felt before. It was his dark angel Suba; he was muscular and dominant. Sally was with her angel who was called Isabella. Suba began to speak to Charles promising him power beyond his comprehension if he would let him have his soul. He was struggling at first, but he could see that Sally and her angel were very seductive.

Suba knew then how to possess his soul. "You know that is Sally's angel, and she hasn't let her take her soul yet. We can persuade her with your help, and we can all have our pleasures together. It doesn't feel good being alone, so come out of your shell and experience something you will never forget." The dark angel teased.

"Yes, yes, please give her to me, and you can have anything you wish of me. I will serve you with all my soul and my mind. Please give me her now, and I am yours forever," Charles said.

Sally thought she was just flirting, but even she realized that she was not in control any more. Her angel did not have her permission to take her soul yet, but now she was beginning to convince her. She put thoughts of passion burning in her mind. Sally was also hesitant; she never thought she would let Isabella finally have her soul. The dark angels cannot take a soul unless they give it freely. She had never felt like this with her husband.

She cried out in a loud voice, "Yes, yes! Please, Isabella, take my soul and have your way with Suba, and let me feel that ecstasy you will feel with him."

Suba and Isabella became entwined. When they were finished with their pleasure of uniting, Charles and Sally came out of their meditations. They began to have intimate relations with each other. Now Satan had Charles and Sally just where he wanted them.

Sally left her husband, and she and Charles lived together. They lived a normal life or so people thought. They were now into the new age movement that was very popular with young college students. They believed they were their own gods now.

Charles had a new spiritual life. He thought he was in charge of his own life. If it felt good to the flesh, the spiritual self would be satisfied. He was going to college to study psychology and wanted to become a professor when he graduated. His dream did come true; he became a professor—the youngest one in the college. Tobit had no idea how much his friend has changed.

The years flew by. Tobit married his high-school sweetheart, Sarah, and had a wonderful life and was blessed with a growing family. Now in his semi-retirement age, he became a CID agent.

The agency needed to fill position for its psychology department. The men and women who work for the agency have gone through some hard times with the stress of the job. Tobit immediately thought of his friend Charles. He knew he was involved in the new age culture, but he heard of his success in his medical career in the psychiatric department of a veterans' hospital in Virginia. He had retired from the college and decided to work part-time at the hospital. He was still with Sally, but they never married, and they still did their meditations. That was how Dr. Charles Booths got started in the agency.

Now the question was, How did the evil one find out that the box was not in the estate's lake? How did they know to try and stop Maria and Robert from finding out what happened to Tobit and Sarah? They did not know that the box was not in the lake, but they did know that as long as the box was supposedly in the lake, it could not free the souls beneath the hospital. And that was why the demons were trying to keep Maria and Robert apart.

Charles befriended Tobit enough to know that he wanted Maria to follow in his footsteps. Charles didn't know how much he was involved with the Secret Service of Angels because Tobit thought his secret was kept from him. But Charles was involved with the fallen angels and had his own suspicions about Tobit. Charles also had his own secret group in the agency that he frequently met up with.

Charles's dark angel appeared to him many times and told him to watch out for Tobit.

The night Tobit went to meet with Michael, Charles kept an eye on him to find out what he was up to. He was unable to see any of the angels on the secret service, but he did notice that Tobit seem to vanish at times as if there was a magical cloak around him. When Tobit was engaged with Michael, he was hidden from sight to protect him. Charles was following him on the night of the accident. He realized he was heading for home, but he noticed it had to be important because he was driving faster than he usually does.

Charles did not see his dark angel as easily as Tobit did his spiritual beings. He would have to do his meditations to communicate with Suba. Charles turned back to his office and began his meditations. While under, he let Suba know that Tobit was heading home rather quickly after making a stop at the hospital. Charles pointed out that he saw Tobit going into the back corridor of the hospital, but when Charles followed him, he vanished. Charles then went back to his car.

A half-hour later, Tobit came out carrying a box. Suba knew that was the box from the fiery wind tornado that the agency was investigating. That was how the demons knew where to find Tobit and tried their hardest to stop him and retrieve the box.

Chapter 8

Time to Free the Trapped Souls

It was time; they all were near the staircase which would lead the holy followers of the Most High to their destiny. As soon as they descended to the lowest level, Robert and Maria could hear the cries and prayers of the souls eagerly waiting to enter their reward in heaven.

Michael let Maria know that her grandmom would be there, but she cannot go to her until the mission was completed. Maria knew this would be so hard for her, but she had the strength to be obedient and has self-control because of the Holy Spirit she received earlier.

No demons could enter the area. When the last angel, Gabriel, descended the stairs, the opening closed shut. Beelzebul knew then they were defeated.

Walking in procession, the angels, Maria, and Robert began to sing praises to God for those souls about to be released to their heavenly reward.

Gabriel held the box open while all were singing. Maria and Robert stood—one on the left and one on the right. The words spoken in unison by the three were not rehearsed because the Spirit of God came upon them.

Amen and Amen.

"Come, dear souls, to your reward with Jesus. His blood was shed for all your sins. You are relieved from any guilt you might have. See them being drawn into the keeper of all your guilt, locked away for all eternity, never to be thought of again. Guardian Angels! Take your places next to those you were assigned to."

Amen and Amen.

Hundreds of souls were guided by their angels to their reward in heaven. Some stayed to join the Secret Service of Angels, waiting for their orders.

Sarah was on the sidelines accompanied by Angel Pamela and Archangel Raphael. Raphael ordered one of the guardian angels leading Jean to her place in heaven to come to see Sarah before she was taken up.

Jean was so overwhelmed with joy to see that Sarah was alive. Raphael gave them a moment to say their goodbyes. Sarah embraced Jean and thanked her for the great sacrifice she made for her and Tobit. Jean was very humbled and most grateful to have Sarah as her sister, and if it weren't for her, Jean's soul would have been lost forever.

Their goodbyes came to an end, and Jean was lifted to heaven. Sarah began to cry because she did not see her beloved husband Tobit.

Raphael turned to Sarah. "Don't worry, Sarah. You will see Tobit in good time. We need all the help we can get to distract the enemy and keep them from this area."

Sarah replied, "I understand, but it has been so long. I know we could never have what we had on earth, but just saying my last goodbye will give me peace."

Suddenly, there was silence. All of the souls have departed. Maria and Robert looked at each other in disbelief. Only a few remained: among them were Sam, Gabriel, Raphael, Pamela, and Sarah.

Maria could not believe who she saw when she turned around: her grandmother.

She ran to her. "Oh, thank God it is you! I've missed you for all these years. It must have been so hard for you to keep silent all that time. Why are you here? How did you know I would be here? Oh,

I have so many questions, but we don't have the time now for me to ask them."

Sarah embraced Maria and understood what she meant.

"We will discuss all your questions after we find out what must be done from Michael."

But Michael was not with them anymore. What was going on now, and where did Michael disappear to?

When Michael was sure all the souls were free, he knew there was trouble behind the hospital. Alexander had summoned him because he and his comrades were in a severe battle with Beelzebul and his team of demons.

They were determined to get the box from Gabriel when they came out of the hospital with Maria and Robert. This time, they were sure to get what they wanted.

Michael showed up, and the battle was won, and the demons hurried away. But Beelzebul stood in front of Michael and told him he would get what he wanted from someone Tobit trusted.

Michael returned to the lower part of the hospital where everyone was eagerly waiting. Robert saw Michael first. The archangel touched Robert's shoulder and told him to go to his room so no one would know that he left. He began to instruct Robert on what was to happen.

"Your parents will be arriving tomorrow to visit you. You will be discharged, and they will take you to the Wright estate because they will be staying there for a few weeks. Sam and his guardian angels will be watching over you. Raphael will also be with you to ensure your speedy recovery."

Then he turned to Maria and the others. "Gabriel, you must take Maria and Sarah back to the estate before the Thompsons return home. But before you get to the house, you must stop at the secret house and place the box in the hidden room. Alexander will be accompanying all of your secret service angels. They will all make camp at Sarah's house until further instruction sometime tomorrow afternoon."

Chapter 9

WHO CAN BE TRUSTED?

Beelzebul had to try a new strategy to get what he wanted. Hopefully, Tobit doesn't suspect his old friend, Charles. Beelzebul knew that those souls were set free, and Tobit would be working with the Secret Service of Angels.

Back at the agency where Charles and his worshipers would have their monthly meetings, chanting could be heard from the evil one. This time, the members would get a response they were not expecting. Suba was so thrilled to take control of Charles. Now Suba's master was allowing him to speak through Charles and submitting other spirits to enter more worshipers at the meeting. It was so horrific that even Sally became frightened. She always enjoyed the pleasures from her dark angel, but she could not imagine them hurting anyone. She and Charles were led by Kundalini, which they thought was the true Holy Spirit, but she was not. Kundalini was an evil spirit to enchant the world with lies.

There was also another group of worshipers at the agency, but they were worshipers of the one true God. And they too received a response, but their response was not from the fake Holy Spirit Kundalini; it was from the third person of the trinity.

After Tobit's death, a new leader was appointed to their group. His name was Nathan Taylor. The group numbered about three hundred men and women. But on the night, there were about thirty who attended the prayer meeting. Nathan was also there with his wife Michell.

Filled with God's Spirit, Nathan began to speak to everyone present. "In the weeks to come, we will complete the mission the Lord gave to Tobit: to return the box which contains the guilt of all humanity to its protected place until it is time to be burned in the fiery punishment with Beelzebul and his legions of followers."

Everyone agreed with a joyful "Amen."

Nathan and Michell lived a few houses away from the Wright's estate. They were home on that terrible night of Tobit and Sarah's so-called accident. Nathan was at the agency when the fiery whirlwind appeared, but he did not go with Tobit that night. When they arrived at the house to find out what happened, they were told it was an act of nature. Sarah wanted to tell them the truth, but she could not let anyone know of her identity.

Nathan rushed to her, "Sarah! Are you okay? Where is Tobit?"

Sarah began to cry but responded, "No I am not…Sarah. I am Jean, her twin sister."

He had never met Jean before and couldn't believe that she wasn't Sarah.

Nathan left the meeting to be by himself and to take in what had just happened. As he prayed, he felt a hand on his shoulder. He knew right away it was the Archangel Michael. And he was willing and ready to listen and be of service.

Michael began to give him instructions. "Peace to you, Nathan, we are continuing the mission from eight years ago. Do you remember hearing about the fiery whirlwind and the container that was given to Tobit? His mission was not completed because of the interference of the evil one.

"Tobit's granddaughter, Maria, and her dear friend Robert have picked up where he and Sarah left off. They found the box and, with the help our Secret Service of Angels and some new recruits, captured the guilt that kept the souls from passing over and set them free. Tobit was among them. He will work as a spirit being instead of a human being.

"I know you have many questions for me, but I will explain more later. Now you and Michell must go to the Wright's estate to help Maria and Robert. But instead of going directly there, go home, give them a call, and invite them over. Just tell them Michael sent you, and they will come right away. Give it two days before you call. Robert will be coming home from the veterans' hospital. You must prepare yourself through fasting and prayer." Michael gave him his blessing.

*****

In the blink of an eye, Maria and Sarah found themselves at Sarah and Tobit's doorstep.

"Grandmom, we are alone now. What are we going to tell everyone? My parents will be home tomorrow, or is it today already? I don't even know what time it is. I hope I remember to call you Aunt Jean," Maria said.

Sarah replied, "Trust me, child, you will find out what we will do in the morning. We need to rest. I know Michael will give us a good excuse to tell your parents, and we will continue our mission later today. Grandpop has a good friend named Charles. He might know something about that night he found the box. He was going to talk to him about what we were involved with, but he wanted to speak to Michael first. I am not sure if he told Michael about him joining our secret group. I can't even talk to Charles because he thinks I am Jean. Well, we will let Michael know what we should do tomorrow. Let's get some needed rest."

*****

Charles did not expect to experience this from his angel, Suba. And Suba reminded Charles that he had his soul, and that meant he had to do what Suba wanted to do. Charles thought he was in control of his life all these years, but now he knew that all his success wasn't his doing. He traded his soul for his fleshly desire which he thought he could never get on his own. Now, he will pay it all back with his soul. He began to fall for new fleshly desires; he felt powerful, and he wanted to have the worshipers at the meeting to show him homage.

At that moment, Suba took complete control, and Charles felt a new ecstasy of power over his people.

He began to quiver with joy, and he said to them, "You will all look upon me. I command you all to summon your angels and give them your souls, and you will all have the spirit of Kundalini. And after we have our fill of ecstasy; we will gladly serve our master, Beelzebul." And that was what they all did in unison.

Now there was a new league of dark angels finally having their way with the humans they were trying to have for so long. Some were young students who followed the professor from the college, and others were from the agency. It started so innocently; they just wanted to experience a peaceful meditation. They were easily caught up in the trend of going against the traditional values which our country was built upon. There was no good or evil, and nothing was sinful in the world as far as they were concerned. Whatever someone felt like doing to themselves was fine as long as no one hurt anyone's feelings. And Mother Nature took the place of God—the creator of all nature. Now they will be slaves of the evil they did not believe in.

All seemed to agree in unison. But there were actually two young men, Nighjal Star and Daymin Taylor, who were not willing to give themselves over to their dark angel. In fact, they were praying to God for help to get them out of this situation. God heard their prayers, and their guardian angel went to battle with their almost dark angels.

In their favor, they both were in the back of the room. With all the excitement going on with the dark angels embracing the human souls, they did not notice the battle going on with the guardian angels. The two young men were cousins, and they were there to spy on this group; they were part of the Secret Service of Angels, and Daymin was Nathan's brother. Nathan had his suspicions about Charles, but Tobit was not sure. Now the question was if Nighjal and Daymin would be able to get free and let Nathan know in time before Charles can be an influence on Maria and Robert.

*****

Suba filled Charles in on what was happening at the Wright estate. "You must befriend Maria and convince her that you were working with Tobit on his last case. Give her your condolences on her grandparents' untimely death, but don't let her know that you know she is trying to find out what happened that horrifying night."

Charles responded, "How can I do that? I just can't go to the house without a reason."

Suba had a plan for Charles. "She will go to the hospital tomorrow with Robert's parents. You just go to your office in the hospital, and you will just happen to cross paths with her."

*****

It was early in the morning, and everyone in the house was still sleeping. Finally, there was some peace at the Wright estate. Alexander was on guard with his fallen heroes; even he thought it was too quiet.

Alexander said to his troops, "Be on watch; it is too still. Joe, you take a few angels and check all around the property."

Joe got right on it and ordered the others to circle the home.

Of course, the first ones to wake up were the McDaniels. They were both eager to see Robert. James went to the kitchen while Rose took a shower.

Sarah heard someone in the kitchen and decided to get out of bed to see who it was. Sarah had a hard time trying to sleep anyway and was also anxious to see Tobit again.

"Oh, hello, James. You remember me? I'm Jean, Sarah's twin sister. How did you get in? And why are you staying here instead of at your house?"

"Oh, Jean. It is so good to see you. Rose and I haven't seen you since that day. We rented our house out when we went to Ireland for a vacation. I don't know if you heard our son Robert was wounded in Afghanistan. Our vacation was cut short, and when we arrived, we realized our house was occupied. So we thought that the Thompsons wouldn't mind if we stayed here until we could check into a hotel. I am sorry if I startled you. We are getting ready to go to the hospital to see him," James responded.

Sarah replied, "Please, you are welcome here anytime. Don't worry about staying at a hotel; you stay here until Robert comes home. Maria did tell me about Robert. We are also going to visit him later on today. I am sorry to hear about your son. Maria did see him yesterday and said he was looking well and was in good spirits."

Just then, Rose came down the stairs and was very surprised and happy to see Jean.

"Oh, Jean! I hope you don't mind us staying. I guess James filled you in on why we are here. Is Maria here? I saw her luggage in one of the rooms. She probably heard about Robert."

"Not at all, Rose, and like I just told James, I am so sorry about Robert. Maria should be down shortly. Let me put on some coffee and make you some breakfast before you go," suggested Sarah.

"If James doesn't mind, I would like that very much. We haven't had anything to eat since our plane trip here yesterday afternoon." Rose looked at James, and he nodded.

Maria awaken by the smell of brewing coffee. With all that she had been through, it gave her a good feeling to wake up to her grandmom's coffee and good breakfast. *Wait*, she thought to herself, *I heard someone talking to Grandmom.* But it didn't sound like her parents. She quickly washed up and went downstairs.

To her surprise, it was Robert's parents.

"Hello, Mr. and Mrs. McDaniel. It is so wonderful to see you again. It has been so long. I am so sorry about Robert. I did see him yesterday, and he was doing very well. I know he can't wait to see you. Jean and I will be stopping by to see him later. Were you here overnight?

They began to share their story with her as they did with Sarah. Sarah served breakfast. After some small talk, James and Rose gave their affectionate goodbyes and told Maria and Jean that they would be back later that day and, hopefully, get to see Gloria and Joseph.

Maria, wondering what time her parents were coming home. She turned to her grandmom. "I should call them to see when they are coming back. Should we wait for them or just go to the hospital?"

Sarah answered, "Give them a call and tell them about Robert and his parents. They might want to come home sooner so they can go and see him too. We have to wait on Michael to find out what we are to do next. We have to act like nothing is going on with our mission."

Maria's phone rang; it was her mother. "Hello, Maria, it's me, mom. Are you okay?"

"Yes, Mom, when are you coming home? Aunt Jean is here too. The McDaniels are staying here as well. Robert was wounded in Afghanistan and is now at the veterans' hospital in Quantico."

Gloria was shocked at the news and told Maria they were leaving the Grossmans' house right away.

Maria and Sarah began to pray together for guidance on an understanding of what would happen to themselves and their family.

Maria asked her grandmom, "How can I go on calling you Jean for the rest of my life? God, please give me courage because this is breaking my heart."

"God will help both of us because I don't know how I can keep from being your grandmom in public. But in our hearts, we know God can do all things. He will be with us forever, my dearest granddaughter."

Maria sighed, "Yes, I know. He has gotten us this far. Jesus, we are only human, and it will be very hard for us to keep hiding our feelings. And we know that only by your mercy and your Holy Spirit are we going to get through it all."

Sarah replied with a humble "Amen." They spent their time in scripture and prayer until Maria's parents came home.

"Be strong. Here they come, 'Aunt Jean'." Maria was ready to play her part.

In came Gloria and Joseph, calling for Maria. "We are home, sweetheart."

"We are in the kitchen, Mom," Maria replied.

Her parents both gave her a hug and kiss and let her know that they hoped all was well with Robert. Gloria turned to Jean and asked her what made her decide to come for a visit. She just did not feel the same being around Jean since the accident.

*****

When Gloria and Joseph arrived at the scene that night, Gloria was devastated to find out that her parents were killed. But when Gloria first saw Jean, she thought she was her mother and for good reason.

She had said, "Mom, what's happening? Where is Daddy?"

Sarah's heart sank into her chest. It took all her strength not to tell her aching daughter the truth. "I…I am so sorry, my dear, but I'm your Aunt Jean. Your mom and dad had a terrible accident."

But when Sarah embraced her daughter, Gloria could not believe that she was not her mother. Her hair was short like Jean's, but something did not seem right.

Late that evening, when the bodies were taken away and all the commotion died down, everyone went to sleep except for Gloria. She noticed the scissors on the kitchen counter with a few strands of hair. She went through the trash and found a small bag of hair clippings. To this day, she kept these clippings but could not get herself to tell Jean. She just couldn't believe her mother would keep something like this from her.

Tobit and Sarah started with the secret service after Gloria went off to college. Gloria knew they were involved in investigations for the CID, but she didn't know anything about the secret agency within the agency because she was so busy with her own life; she never seemed interested in what her parents were involved with, especially if it didn't involve her.

Sarah tried to share some of her work with Gloria. For instance, she would ask her to go with her on her photo-shooting adventures and tried to encourage her daughter to take photography classes in college, but Gloria just couldn't get into it. She just wanted to do her own thing, like most college-age girls do. But as she grew older, she wished she did more things with her parents, especially her mom. After having her own family, she understood what she was missing with her mom. Would she ever confront "Jean" about her suspicions all these years, or would she just trust what Jean had told her knowing in her heart that it wasn't true?

*****

Sarah was almost at a loss for words.

But Maria interrupted, "Oh, Mom, I asked her to come down and spend some time with us. And I thought she would want to see Robert. I hope you don't mind. I know we are busy trying to get the house ready for sale." She took her mom aside and whispered to her, "I really think Jean should face what happened and be at peace with herself."

Her mom agreed and left it at that. Jean suggested that they freshen up, then she would make them some lunch before they all go over to see Robert and his parents. And that was what everyone did.

Jean rented a car, and Maria told her mom she would go with Jean to the hospital because they might come home a little later that night. Gloria wondered why, but she didn't question them. Never knowing what to expect from Michael, Maria thought she would drive separate from her parents. They would be late, but Michael would not be the reason.

Maria and Sarah left first. When they arrived at the hospital, they would have to pass by Charles's office. And he made sure he would be there to meet Maria and Sarah before they saw Robert. Charles was also leaving his house to go to his office at the hospital. But the leader of the fallen angels had other ideas of how to get Jean's trust in Charles than he did; if Jean saw Charles in need of help from an accident, she would get to know him better.

About three miles from the hospital, Charles's tire blew out, and his car swerved into a ditch. He was so upset because he thought he would not meet Jean and Maria. He put his hazard lights on and got out of the car to fix his flat. He put out some flares on the road to avoid an accident.

Sarah and Maria just happened to approach Charles's car. Maria told her grandmom to pull over to see if someone needed help, and they did pull over in front of Charles's car. He was becoming very angry about what was happening and began swearing as he was getting the spare tire out from under his car. He thought to himself as he saw the car pull up, *Really? I know how to fix this. I will just wave them to move on. I don't have time to chat with anyone. I have to get to the hospital so I don't miss my opportunity to meet with Jean and Maria.* He walked over to the car to tell them he was okay, but to his surprise, he recognized Jean.

Sarah got out of the car and, not knowing at first who he was, spoke to him, "We just wanted to make sure you were okay. Charles, is that you? I have not seen you since the funeral. We were just heading to the hospital to see a dear friend of ours."

Charles replied, "Well, well, Jean. This is a pleasure. I was just heading over to the hospital too. I work there as a psychologist. Maybe we can get together after you visit your friend. I hope he is well enough to be released soon. Please stop by my office before you go home."

Sarah was hoping Charles would not find out her identity. Tobit had tried to get the real Jean and him to go out with each other. They might have had a few dates, and Sarah was hoping he would not bring up anything she wouldn't had known about.

"This is Maria, my niece. We would love to see you after we visit Robert." Sarah and Maria returned to their car and continued toward the hospital.

"Grandmom, you're not considering telling him any about our mission, are you? I am not sure if he can be trusted."

She replied, "I am thinking about it. Grandpop had mentioned it to me before, that he was considering asking Charles to join the secret service. But he wanted to clear it with Michael. They had been friends since high school. Maybe he might be of some help in finding out who was spying on Tobit that night."

Maria didn't feel the same about her grandmom's decision. She was hoping Michael would agree.

They finally arrived at the hospital. When Maria was passing by Charles's office, she thought she saw someone there in the corner of her eye. But when she went to look, there was no one. The Holy Spirit had given Maria a gift of discernment, and she was certain that Charles has a dark side.

She was right; there was something waiting in his office to make sure that Charles would intervene and work his way into their confidence. And now, they knew that Maria would interfere with their plans, and they would have to get Jean alone with Charles. But how?

Robert was sitting up in his hospital bed. Having his parents at his side gave him great pleasure and comfort. He was grateful that his parents were not grieving over his death. Robert let them know that Sam was a hero and that he was with Jesus in heaven. Rose and James loved Sam as their own son. Sam had no one to claim his body, so they would claim his body and give him a proper burial. Robert was feeling so blessed that his parents would do this for Sam because he loved Sam as a brother.

Joseph and Gloria were also visiting Robert. They told him Maria would be there shortly with her Aunt Jean. Just then, in they came, and Maria went up to Robert and gave him a tender embrace. Sarah patiently waited for her turn and gave Robert a hug.

A nurse came into the room to remind his guests that only three at a time can visit.

Gloria said, "Okay, Maria. You and your father can come with me to get some coffee in the cafe."

That would leave Sarah alone with Rose and James. Maria didn't want to leave Sarah, but she told her they would be leaving when she comes back.

An emergency alarm went off. There were wounded coming in from the helipad on the roof. The visitors were told on the loud-speaker to keep the corridors clear until the emergency is contained. Charles was already in the hospital and right next to Robert's room, and he had to go in because it was the nearest room.

Sarah was not expecting to see Charles again so soon, and she thought it was a sign that maybe she should trust him.

"Oh, Jean, what a pleasure to see you again. Where is Maria?" He was happy not to see her there; he can now have Jean to himself.

Sarah answered, "Maria and her parents went to get coffee. Charles, this is Robert McDaniel and his parents, James and Rose."

"It is nice to meet you. I think we have met before at the funeral for Mr. and Mrs. Wright. Tobit and I go all the way back from high school."

"Oh yes," replied Rose. "I remember seeing you there, but we were not properly introduced. It is good to meet you."

Charles turned to Robert. "Thank you, Robert, for serving our country. You have grown into a fine young man. You know, my office is down the hall. If you need to talk, I am here for you. Here is my card. I am the psychologist for the veterans' hospital."

Charles now had his chance to see Jean alone. "Jean, what do you say coming with me for a bite to eat down the road? I am sure Maria won't mind going home with her parents. And I can bring you back to your car after."

Sarah was a little hesitant at first. But she told Robert to tell Maria she had to leave and gave him her car keys to give to Maria so she could take it back to the house. The alarm went off again, and an announcement on the speaker told everyone it was clear go back to the corridors. Charles made sure they left before Maria and her parents got back.

Charles told Sarah he had to go back to his house to pick up something. "Do you mind if I stop at the house first? I had left some papers I needed for my office."

She replied, "Sure, not at all, Charles."

He held her hand, and they began to walk toward his car. Like a gentleman, he opened the car door for her.

Sarah started to have feelings she had not had since she was with Tobit. She thought she was too old to start having that kind of feeling she felt when he held her hand. Just maybe they could be involved and continue with the mission together. She did not know Charles was living with Sally, and he was not going to tell her about it. In fact, he had an apartment that Sally didn't even know about; he would have some young women from the nearby college come over for his meditation lessons, as he called them.

They arrived at Charles's apartment. Then he asked Sarah if she would like to come in. He had no intention of going out for a bite; he had other plans for Sarah.

Charles let her inside and asked, "Jean, instead of going out, why don't I order us some Chinese food? You remember out first date? We had Chinese. But this time, I will not be as shy as I was then."

Sarah remembered Jean talking about that night with Charles. She did tell her how shy he was, and she thought it was kind of cute, but they never really clicked together. There was something about Charles that Sarah found attractive. He was still a very attractive man and was physically fit for his age.

"Well, okay, I don't want Maria to worry about me. But I don't think she'll mind."

"Jean, time has been good to you. You are as attractive as you were that night. I wish we would have been more than friends. Maybe now we can work on it. I am glad I had the flat tire, or I would have never met you again." He moved closer to Sarah, and he thought to himself, *Well, I don't think I will need anything to get her in the mood. The more natural I am, the more she will trust me.*

Sarah *was* caught up in the moment. Charles began to put his arms around Sarah and caressed her hair and touched her face. Then his lips kissed her forehead and made their way to her lips.

It has been so long for Sarah; she just wanted more from Charles. She was very vulnerable and didn't want him to stop. She kissed him back, and they both began to have the relationship Charles wanted. He didn't even have to use his tricks to convince her.

Sarah's ecstasy was more than she could imagine. She was ready to tell Charles everything and have him join the secret service. She did feel guilty for what had happened, but in her mind, she was ready to make a commitment with Charles like she had with Tobit.

"Charles, I want to tell you something. Tobit wanted to let you in on the secret work he was involved with. And I think he was right. You have made me feel so passionate tonight; I can't explain it. It was so wonderful."

Charles just looked tenderly into Sarah's eyes and began to make love to her again.

Sarah fell for his charms and began telling him everything. She stayed with him all night.

The next day, while she was still in his bed, she woke up to the smell of a good breakfast that Charles made for her. He came into the room and began to kiss her. After caressing some more, she showered up, and they had breakfast.

She thought that if she was going to stay with Charles, she should tell him who she really was. "Charles, I have to tell you something else. But you have to swear to not tell anyone. I am not Jean; I am Sarah, Tobit's wife. And I know I should not have a relationship with you yet, but I hope we can have more than this."

Charles could not believe how easy it was for this to happen. He almost felt guilty because he was really having feelings for her. He had never felt this way before; it felt real. There were no gimmicks, no meditation. He wanted Sarah too as much as she did him. He wasn't shy; he had never felt so comfortable with anyone before. What was happening to him, and how could he fix it? Has he gone so far that he could not get out of his contract with Suba? Should he tell Sarah and ask for help, or is it hopeless?

"I hope you do not think I am that kind of woman who get involved with anyone. I can't explain what happened; I let my guard down. It has been so long since anyone embraced me the way you have. Maria told me not to trust you. I hope I have not jeopardized our mission by telling you. How do you feel now that you know I am not Jean? Did you have feelings for her like this?"

Charles took her in his arms. "You know, Sarah, I really wanted to know you instead of your sister. But I didn't want to let Tobit know how I felt. And I was very shy, and I tried to talk to you at school, but I never could. And you know, I did kiss Jean. Well, she kissed me, but there was nothing. Kissing you, that felt different. I can't explain how it felt. It was so real like it was meant to be. Last night was special, and I never want that feeling to end.

"Sarah, I have to tell you something too. I don't know where to start. If you don't feel the same after I tell you, I'll understand." He then told her everything even about Sally. He told Sarah about how Sally got him into the Kundalini meditations and that being with her didn't make him feel selfish; he just felt peaceful and wanted to give her joy instead of just pleasing himself. It wasn't about his ego or his own ecstasy; it must really be what God intended relationships to be.

He also admitted that he was trying to lure her into his apartment just to get her to trust him. "Sarah, I am the one who betrayed Tobit. And I am a leader of the occult group at the agency. How do I get out of this situation? If this dark angel is part of me, where is he now? There is no way he would let me talk to you like this. Maybe there is a chance I can get my soul back. Please, Sarah, believe me. Maybe that is why we met; you must help me. Suba is so strong, and I don't know how to send him back to where he came from."

"Why don't we pray together for forgiveness and ask for guidance on what we can do? Do you believe that Jesus died for our sins and rose again so that we could have victory over death and eternal life with him? From what you have told me, it has been a long time since you have had God in your life. For some reason, God has brought us together, and his angel must be protecting you right now from Suba. Please, Charles, just ask for God's mercy. And just like in the book of Jonah, the people of Nineveh, and God did not destroy them. I think Tobit knew that deep inside, you were crying out for help. He is praying for you at this moment, and that is why Suba can't reach you now. The power of God is greater than his. Don't be frightened; I am here to support you."

Charles began to weep bitterly and cried out, "Yes, Sarah, I do believe. Please, let's pray together. And please forgive me too for deceiving you by bringing you here to spy on you." He took Sarah's hands, and they both began to pray. They prayed, first of all, for the forgiveness of their sins. Sarah pleaded for the Archangel Michael to appear to them both and lead them in victory against Suba and his follower of dark angels.

Chapter 10

The Battle for Innocent and Naive Souls

There was a good reason for why Suba was not with Charles. After the souls were recovered, there was still much work to do for the guardian angels.

The archangels were alerted that there were hundreds of new dark angels summoned from the agency.

Gabriel turned to Sam. "You must lead your guardian angels to the agency as soon as possible. We have to save as many souls as we can. Prepare for battle!"

Suba had to leave Charles because Beelzebul called all the available dark angels back to save the new dark angels that were summoned. Suba felt like Charles had Jean just where he wanted her. But thank God, Sarah had Charles just where she wanted him, and God had Sarah and Charles where He wanted them.

Maria felt helpless not knowing what was happening with her grandmom. She stayed with Robert after everyone had left.

The doctor came into the room hoping to see his parents, but he just missed them.

"Good evening, Robert, I am not sure if you remember me. My name is Dr. David Pompeii. I was hoping your parents would be here. I am sorry for visiting you so late, but we had a few emergencies tonight. And who is this young lady?"

Robert answered, "She is a dear friend of mine, Second Lieutenant Maria Thompson."

She extended her hand to the doctor. "Pleasure to meet you, Dr. Pompeii. When can Robert go home?"

He replied, "Yes, good news for you both. You have had a miraculous recovery. You can be discharged tomorrow."

Maria asked the doctor, "Doctor, is there any way Robert can go home tonight? I am his senior officer, and I will sign him out and make sure his unit gets contacted."

He seemed hesitant but replied, "You know, that might be good for his morale. Here is Dr. Charles Booth's card. You have been through a very traumatic experience. I strongly suggest you make an appointment with him. Even though you are physically ready to go home, you are not ready to go into any combat duty until you see our psychiatrist. So, Second Lieutenant, you are responsible for Corporal McDaniel getting the care he will need."

Maria replied, "Yes, Dr. Pompeii, I will make sure he does. Thank you so much for releasing him into my custody."

Dr. Pompeii said, "You are very welcome. But don't forget to see Dr. Booths. It is very important."

When the doctor left the room to sign Robert out, Maria gave Robert a tender caress and kissed him then let him know she was very concerned about her grandmom. She hadn't heard from her since yesterday.

"Let's get you home, and we will see if we can find out what Michael has in store for us now. I am going to try and call my grandmom."

Robert began to get ready and pack his bag. The nurse came in and told Robert to sign the release form and that he was ready to go.

Just as they were ready to leave, Michael appeared to them.

"I see you are ready to go home. I will meet you in the parking lot. There are some gentlemen from our agency whom you must meet. He was going to call on you at your house tomorrow, but things have changed. You will need all the help you can get. There's a battle going on in the CID agency with guardian angels and the dark angels. They need the archangels' assistance. Alexander and his company and others will help you as needed."

Robert replied, "Okay, Michael. We will be right out."

Maria interrupted him and began speaking to Michael. "Please, Michael, is my grandmother okay with Charles?"

"Yes, Maria, she is found. Don't worry. God is in control of everything,"

They went out into the parking lot. Michael had two of Tobit's friends from the secret agency, Nighjal and Daymin, who managed to escape from the satanic group the night before. Michael introduced them to Maria and Robert.

Nighjal started to say, "Nice to meet you both. We do have some news about Charles."

Before he could finish talking, Michael interrupted him. "Listen, Nighjal and Daymin, before you tell them about Charles. I want to let you now that Charles is about to come over to our side, but he will need all of our help. Right now, the demons are not watching over him because of the battle going on at the agency. I should be there myself now, but I want you all to make sure Sarah and Charles are protected. Alexander and his company should be here any minute. They will protect you all until we gather up these dark angels and send them to their eternal punishment."

Daymin looked at Nighjal with disbelief. "Wow, Charles looked so far gone. I didn't think he could be saved."

Michael touched Nighjal and Daymin on their shoulders. "Being human, your sins may increase, but God's mercy is overflowing. No one can take your soul because God created it. Humans do have free will to accept their destiny in heaven or hell."

Nathan pulled into the lot and got out of is car to meet Nighjal and Daymin. His brother had called him to meet with them to tell him about Charles. He was surprise to see Michael there with Maria and Robert.

"Well, I thought I was just meeting with Daymin and Nighjal. Michael, this must be very important. Have we changed our plans about meeting tomorrow? Is this little Maria Thompson? You have grown into a beautiful young woman. And you must be Robert

McDaniel. I am proud of you and am glad to hear how well you have recovered from your accident in Afghanistan."

He then looked over at Daymin and asked, "What news did you hear that was so important you could not tell me on the phone?'

Daymin sighed. "The news has changed a little. Michael will clue you in on what's happening."

Michael began to tell him the story of the cult having their meeting which turned out to be a revival for Satan and his dark angels and about how Charles was in charge of that meeting. Now Charles no longer wanted to be a part of it.

"The dark angel was supposed to be watching over Charles while Suba was summoned to help defeat our guardian angels. But they were captured and sent to their untimely end by Alexander. Then Charles was freed to make his own decision to follow Jesus with the help of Sarah."

Daymin replied, "I know God is merciful, but with what Nighjal and I witnessed, it is so hard to believe that there was any hope for his salvation or for any of the worshipers. And I know what you are thinking, Michael; if He could forgive Nineveh in the time of Jonah, there is hope for all mankind."

Michael confirmed with a smile on his face. "Yes, Daymin, that was what I was thinking."

Now it was time for Michael to give orders to everyone.

"Maria and Robert, go to Tobit's estate and wait there until the archangels and I take victory over the current battle. Nathan, you take Daymin and Nighjal back to your house. Put your armor of prayer on to get ready for our mission. Alexander and company will surround the estate. And Alexander, get ahold of Pamela so she can be with Sarah. Also summon Charles's guardian angel to prepare for the battle to protect his soul. As soon as we defeat the dark angel, Raphael will help Charles cross over." Michael prayed over the group and gave them his blessing.

Everyone left the lot, ready to do their part. Maria and Robert were on their way to her grandparents' house. Daymin and Nighjal decided to go home first and pack a few things before going to Nathan's house. Alexander and his company headed to guard and protect the family and friends at the Wright estate. And he called on Pamela and commanded some of his angels including Charles's guardian angel, Thomas, to watch over him. Thomas had not been called to guide Charles since he gave himself to Suba. Thomas had been in deep prayer for all those years so that Charles would come to God, and soon, his vigilant prayers would be answered.

*****

Sarah and Charles were deep in prayer. They both felt some guilt for having a sexual relationship before even getting to know each other. Charles took Sarah in his arms and told her he was sorry if she thought he was taking advantage of her.

Sarah said, "You did not take advantage of me. I willingly gave myself to you because your tender touch was what I thought I need at that time, and I want it to continue forever, but I am willing to wait until God unites us together."

Charles gave her a gentle kiss. Looking into her eyes, he said, "I do not want this feeling to end either. I want to make love to you right now, but I know you are right. I have been living in the flesh for too long; now I want to give myself to God. And I will wait until He unites us with His blessing."

They both felt at peace with themselves. God was now listening to their prayer of commitment. And at that, Thomas touched Charles's shoulder ready to protect his soul and his new commitment to serve God with the help of the true Holy Spirit.

Pamela had just arrived at Charles's apartment waiting for the moment to talk to Sarah and Charles after both prayed for a sign from God.

Pamela then came in and called to Sarah. "Sarah, God has heard your prayers. He has sent me and the fallen heroes from Alexander's company. We are here to protect you and Charles from the dark angels."

"Thank God you are here, Pamela. What is going on? Where is Michael? We need him here with us."

Charles was taken by surprise because he had never seen an angel from God. And he felt a little guilty because he felt so unworthy after all the evil he had done against God.

Pamela turned to Charles. "God has forgiven you, Charles. Tobit is with Michael now defeating your dark angel Suba and the other dark angels at the agency. He has been praying for you, and now his prayers have been answered."

Sarah excused herself from the room. "Charles, I'll be right back. I just want to have a word with Pamela in private."

Thomas then turned to Sarah an explained, "We have a few things to talk about, Sarah. You go and talk to Pamela while I fill Charles in on why we are here."

Sarah went into the next room, and Pamela followed. "What is wrong, Sarah? Is it because of Tobit?"

"Yes, Pamela, I feel like I broke my promise to Tobit to be ever-faithful. And I haven't even seen him yet to tell him how much I have missed him and still love him."

Pamela took hold of Sarah's hand. "Sarah, please don't feel guilty. Tobit knows you are lonely. What you had with Tobit on earth was wonderful, and now he wants you to be happy and have a new life to share with someone else. You will see him soon, and he will let you know that he wants the best for you and Charles."

*****

After Charles left the agency a few days ago, he thought everyone had also left to go to their homes, but Daymin's and Nighjal's guardian angel could not let all those people's souls get taken, so they united with the other guardian angels to fight back and help the ones who were misled.

Sam, the new leader for the guardian angels, called on Michael for reinforcements. Sam knew the evil forces held at this meeting was very powerful. Of course, the guardian angels could have the dark angels fleeing, but they would just return at another time to feast on the humans' fleshly desires and take control of their souls. Only the archangels can send them to their eternal punishment before the end of time. Sam had to make sure that none of them should flee the building.

The battle was so strong and lasting longer than it should have. That was why Beelzebul was called and had Suba, Isabella, and the other dark angels to come to the battle. It had to be serious enough to leave Charles and Sally, giving them a chance to change their hearts and let the true Spirit of God into their hearts if they chose to.

Sam cried out to God for help, pleading for the Archangel Michael to appear. In an instant, Michael was there, speaking to Sam.

"I am here. You have led your command into victory. Gabriel and Raphael have surrounded the perimeter of the dark angels. Where is Tobit? He must leave and protect Maria and Robert at the estate."

Sam was so grateful to see Michael and replied, "Thank God, Michael, you are here. We have tried so hard not to allow any of them to escape from here. I knew that Beelzebul is a very powerful demon, and Tobit was trying to get his attention so we could keep our battle going strong until you and your angels come to finish the job. Tobit knew Beelzebul would be looking for him because he interfered with his plans to control the box. Tobit shouted out to Beelzebul to fight him. They went into the next room. I think he needs some help; I haven't seen him for a while now."

"Do you think you can hold them down for ten minutes, Sam? I will see if he needs my help. Well, I am sure he does need my help; he is new at this."

Sam agreed, "Yes, Michael, please hurry!"

Beelzebul couldn't kill Tobit again, but he could weaken him enough to be helpless to continue the battle. And that was exactly what he had done.

"Now, Tobit, I will continue the fight and strengthen my dark angels. You are not strong enough to defeat me any longer. I have taken care of you and Sarah before, but this time, I will be victorious and control the thoughts of this nation."

Beelzebul continued to weaken Tobit with his words of hopelessness until Tobit fell to his knees in despair.

The moment Tobit fell, Michael was there to help him up.

"Get on your feet, Tobit. Raphael will be here soon. I will take care of Beelzebul."

Beelzebul began to speak to Michael, "This is not your battle. Let Tobit fight his own battle. What are you doing interfering with my worshiper? The humans came here on their own free will. Tobit cannot save his friend Charles. He is mine now. Suba made sure of it and took full possession of him. Tobit's prayers were wasted all these years."

Michael spread his wings. And Beelzebul became intimidated by Michael's epic appearance.

Michael raised his voice and pronounced, "You have no power over God's creatures, both human and spiritual. If one does not deny the Holy Spirit, God will not deny his mercy to anyone. Beelzelbul! My angels and the other archangels have given your dark angels their final condemnation, and the humans and their souls were set free. Now, be gone from this place until your time of condemnation!"

Raphael guided Tobit to another room in the agency.

He laid his hands on Tobit and spoke to him, "Tobit, God has given me the power to give you strength to continue your mission. You will be even stronger and will not fall to your knees again because of Beelzebul. You must go now to Sarah and give her your okay for her to move on with her new life with Charles. You must keep praying for Charles because Beelzebul is determined to bring him back to his flock of worshipers."

Tobit became strong and assumed a form similar to an angelic being. "What has happened to me? I feel transformed into a new person. Would Sarah and the others recognize me? I do not feel worthy of such an honor. Thank you, Raphael. What is my role now? To finish the job we had started many years ago?"

Raphael replied, "Gabriel will fill you in on what you are to do. Go now to see Sarah, and all of you will be guided from there." He withdrew from Tobit.

In an instant, Tobit was transported to Charles's apartment where Sarah was confiding in Pamela.

Tobit materialized in front of Sarah's eyes. Pamela gave them both their privacy and went into the next room with Charles and Thomas, the guardian angel.

Sarah didn't recognize Tobit at first because of his new spiritual form. "Tobit, is that you?"

He replied, "Yes, Sarah, it's me. The Archangel Raphael prayed over me, and the Lord transformed me to give me more strength to stand against the evil one. I miss you, Sarah. You have given me everything and more in our lives together. We had a beautiful little daughter. It must have been so painful for her to find out her parents were killed and more grievous for you to pretend to be Jean.

"Our secret work has been passed on to our granddaughter, Maria. Our little Gloria just wasn't interested in what we were involved with, but I know she regrets keeping us out of her adult life. After this mission is complete, I think she should know the truth. You are not aware of this, but Gloria found your hair clippings that night, and she did not let you know about it.

"You have suffered for too long with this secret of deception and also from being alone and single. I want you to be happy. Raphael filled me in about you and Charles. Yes, Sarah, it is time for you to move on. It doesn't mean that I don't love you anymore, but 'death did us part'. And now, I am a spiritual being, and you have a long life ahead of you. You and Charles have may blessing to move on together."

Sarah touched Tobit's hand and brought it to her cheek. "Thank you, Tobit. I know now that I am ready to take the next step in my life. And about Gloria… I had my suspicions that she didn't believe me when I told her I was Jean. She is stronger than I thought because she has kept that from me. It's like she knows she's protecting me from someone. I want to let her know somehow that I am so proud of her."

This was the closure Sarah needed to help her go forward in her new life.

It was time to complete their mission. Everyone would do their part to throw Beelzebul on the wrong track so that Maria and Robert would succeed. Everyone was where they had to be for now. It was a long and challenging day, but it was time for everyone to rest for tonight. Tomorrow, they would need to be strong in their faith so God would give them victory.

*****

Maria and Robert surprised his parents when they got home from the hospital. Rose and James could not believe their son was safe and at home with them. And Daymin and Nighjal stayed at Nathan and Michell's house near the Wright estate. All the fallen heroes, guardian angels, and archangels were at their assigned posts for the night. All seemed quiet for now.

One by one, everyone came down for breakfast. This time, Maria and Robert were up and making breakfast for the entire group.

Rose woke up first. "I should be making you breakfast, son. You should be resting. Your father and I are going to do some errands this afternoon. I hope you don't mind."

James then chimed in. "Yes, we do, son. But we will spend more time with you tomorrow. We've missed you so much. I hope you have enough leave because we have so much to catch up on. Are you sure you are okay? It's a miracle that you have recovered so quickly. You were in a coma for so long; we thought the worst. We are so thankful God has answered our prayers."

Robert went over to his parents and embraced them. "I am okay, thank God. And thanks to Maria for being by my side." Then he turned to Gloria and Joseph and gave them a hug too. He let them know how much he appreciated their daughter's help.

Gloria then turned to Maria. "Where is your Aunt Jean? I haven't seen her since yesterday. Is she visiting with someone?"

Maria answered, "Yes, she is, Mom. Do you remember grandpa's friend Charles Booths? She saw him at the hospital when we visited Robert. I am sorry I didn't tell you earlier, but I just found out myself not too long ago. She texted me and told me she was staying at his place, and she will let me know when she will be home. But I have not heard from her since."

Gloria looked a little worried about the situation. "Yes, I do know Charles. I had only seen him a few times when I was very little. I didn't know Jean knew him." Then she turned to Robert. "I am sorry, Robert; I was not ignoring you. I was just concerned about what happened to her. It's not like her to go off like that without letting anyone know where she is going. Joseph and I are very relieved that you are safe and with us and your family. And I am so happy that you and Maria are finally together after all these years."

James and Rose asked Gloria and Joseph if they would like to join them; they were just checking to make sure their house was okay. They wanted to let the tenants know they came home early, and they did not have to leave because Rose and James have decided to stay at a hotel until their lease was up. They would then head to the mall afterward to pick up a few things. It would give them all the time to do some catching up. Joseph and Gloria agreed because they thought Maria and Robert needed some time to themselves as well.

That was very true; they had a job to do, and this would give them the alone time they needed.

Robert said, "You guys go ahead. Don't worry about us; we have a lot of catching up to do too. We love you. And if we are not here when you get back, please don't get upset. We will be back."

Their parents seemed a little hesitant, but they decided to leave them alone, no questions asked.

*****

Robert would be stationed in a county called Prince Williams, near the Marine Corps base, at Quantico. It was in that small town where the commander of a group of guardian angels was getting ready to help complete this mission. Her name was Heather. She was the highest-ranking angel in the region. The angels who were under her command would shield Maria and Robert and everyone else against Beelzebul and his demon troops. God had given those under her command the power to blind the enemy from seeing them. They became the same type of guardian angels who, in the scriptures, led Saint Paul and also Saint Peter out of prison undetected by the guards.

Heather was one of the youngest heroes of the War of Independence. Her sister Linda was also a heroine. They were taking care of the injured soldiers. The enemy was getting too close to the first aid unit, so Heather and Linda disguised themselves as male soldiers. A few other women joined them to draw the British soldiers away from the injured soldiers. When they were a safe distance away, they began to fire their muskets. The British were convinced that the colonists had changed directions. Finally, the injured soldiers were rescued. There were twenty-five women in that battle led by the two brave sisters. Even though the sisters were casualties, the women took victory in the battle for freedom.

Once again, these two sisters will confuse the enemy, but Linda will have her own group of guardian angels across the Potomac River. Now, the evil one knew that the power of the box would be protected on a body of water, and they also knew of Heather and Linda guarding the Potomac River. Beelzebul decided to have his demons spy around that area. That was what the Archangel Michael wanted him to think.

The archangels gathered together to plan what would happen next.

"The enemy will be watching every move that Maira and Robert make," Michael said to Gabriel and Raphael. "They do not suspect Sarah of returning the box to its proper dwelling place. As far as they know, Sarah passed over with Tobit. Gabriel, you go to Sarah and Charles and guide them to where the box is at Sarah's secret hideaway. Raphael and I will go to Maria and Robert and to the Taylor brothers and Nighjal. Heather, Linda, and their guardian angels are going to guide Sarah and Charles to their destination undetected by the fallen angels. And when the evil one has been misled, we will come together to witness the return of the box."

Chapter 11

Will Charles Give His Soul Back to Beelzebul to Save a Friend?

When Gabriel arrived at Charles's apartment, he saw Sarah with Pamela. Sarah was very upset, and Gabriel began to question why she looked so sad.

"Sarah, why do you worry so? Where are Charles and Thomas? Thomas was told to keep watch on Charles. I was sent by Michael to prepare you for your mission. You are the one who will return the box. You and Charles have to go to retrieve the box from its hiding place. We will trust God with this plan, and we will be victorious. Now tell me, what exactly happened here?"

Sarah handed Gabriel a letter that Charles left her.

> Dearest Sarah,
>
> There is something I have to do before we make our commitment to each other. Sally is coming home today. I want to tell her in person that I am ending our relationship. To be honest, it should have ended many years ago, but that is another story I won't go into now. Also, I am hoping that she would want to repent and reject

> Isabella. I hope I am not too late. I tried to leave quietly, but Thomas was alert and tried to stop me. He couldn't keep me here against my will, so he went with me.
>
> Love you, my darling,
> Charles

"I am sure Charles is being tested by God. We have to make sure he can be trusted. Pamela, you take Sarah to where she hid the box. Heather, Linda, and some of their guardian angel company will meet you there. The enemy will not be watching Sarah because they still believe she is Jean. Their angels can't be seen by the fallen angels. Don't worry about Charles. Thomas will guide him if he passed his test of worthiness.

"Sarah, please do not be in anguish over Charles. You must be focused on your mission. I am sure he will be ready in time to return this box before it can fall into the wrong hands. Tobit will be there when the event happens. His job will be essential. Once we get to the destination. Tobit will be lifted up to bring the box to its proper place. It is fitting for such a hero as Tobit to be the guardian of such a valuable instrument until the final days."

Sarah was awed by what was said to her by Gabriel. "I am so humbled and honored to be a part of what is to happen. I love Tobit with all my heart. I will miss him, and I am deeply proud that he will serve our God with this most noteworthy role. I am ready to serve as well. Let us go now with the blessing of the Lord."

*****

Thomas spoke to Charles before he went in to see Sally. "Charles, I will give you your privacy with Sally. You will not be able to see me, but I will be nearby to protect you. Remember to keep your guard against the enemy. I can't control your will, so seek out God's truth for you. Go, you have my blessing."

Charles was not aware of God testing him. He asked Thomas to please pray for him because he knew he was vulnerable to Sally's charms. He also knew he had to do this for Sarah.

Charles walked up the path to his house. He knew Sally was there because her car was in the driveway. Then he turned back to see if Thomas was there, and he was nowhere in sight. Just as Thomas told him, *Yes, Lord, I am ready to do what I think is right for Sarah and for You,* he thought.

He called out to Sally when he opened the door. "Are you home, Sally? It's me. Please come downstairs I have something to tell you." He didn't get an answer and began to be concerned.

Sally was upstairs, but she wasn't alone. There was a demon of self-destruction hovering over her shoulder as she prepared to give herself a fix. Charles had no idea that Sally was involved with drugs.

"What are you doing? Did you ask this demon to be a part of your life? You always told me meditation was better than taking drugs. Why?"

The demon went between them as Charles got closer to Sally. "Your Sally has been doing this for at least two years now. And you know what?" He paused with an evil laugh. "This time, it will be her last fix. That syringe in her hand has more than what her body can handle. Yes, Charles, she wants a permanent end.

"Have you heard about Suba, your dark angel that has given you such pleasure and power? He was destroyed, and rumor has it that you betrayed him and decided to go over to our enemy. Well, now, Beelzebul won't have it. He said you made a commitment with him long ago when you and Sally were craving each other. You remember that night? She came to your place. You were so innocent. Never been with a woman, just the way Suba liked his intended host; you think you can get out of selling your soul for this woman that easily. Tell you what, Charles, I'll let her live if you agree to host a new dark angel. He is even more handsome than Suba, and he will make you feel thirty years younger.

"But Sally…she's not as hot as your new friend Jean, is she? Don't worry, Sally is too stoned to hear us. Maybe you can get Jean to make a commitment with an attractive dark angel. You help us get that box, and Sally won't die tonight. And you and your new chick will enjoy the rewards. Or if you don't want to involve her, you can have Merit, the darkest angel, all to yourself. You will not get out of this house alive, and neither will Sally if you don't let him have you now."

Charles was surrounded by guilt from the angels of guilt and despair. He was starting to agree with him. He didn't want Jean involved with it. He had to try and save Sally before it was too late.

Just as he was reaching out to Merit, Beelzebul was so anxious; he appeared too soon and was going to let Sally overdose. Charles realized that trying to save Sally was not going to happen. Beelzebul had no need for her anymore. Charles ran to save Sally from taking her fix by pulling the needle out of her hands. He realized he was now a child of God. With all the strength that he had, he stood up to Beelzebul and the dark angels, then he shielded Sally from them. He began to beg God's forgiveness and prayed in Jesus's name to come to his rescue.

Thomas was there to battle the demons that were ready to attack Sally and Charles, but he was not alone because Merit was so strong and one of the darkest of all the dark angels. The Archangel Raphael was side by side with Thomas because only an archangel could fight against Beelzebul.

Beelzebul retreated from Charles and Sally's house, but Merit and the other demons were cast down to their eternal punishment. Raphael touched Charles's shoulder and let him know of his heroic act to save Sally.

Sally was not comprehensive of her surroundings. "Charles, what just happened? You just knocked me over. I thought I was having a bad nightmare, or was it real? Oh, I am so sorry about all this. I guess you now know about my habit. Charles, I need something really bad. I only had enough for one fix, and you took it from me." She began to scream at him.

He told her about everything that happened.

She then told him, "Why didn't you just take the damn dark angel?"

Charles replied with patience because he knew she was not herself, "Please, Sally, listen. Beelzebul was going to let you die because that shot would have given you an overdose."

He then asked Thomas and Raphael to give him some privacy, just for a few minutes. They agreed and went downstairs.

"Sally, I have to tell you something. We've known for a while now that our relationship was ending. But I want you to know I will care for you as a friend and a friend who needs my help. Why did you turn to drugs?"

Sally finally composed herself and began to speak, "Yes, I have known it was over between us. And I have been cheating on you for over two years now. I met someone who was into drugs to enhance his spiritual relationship with his dark angel. His name is Troy.

"I had to have more satisfaction, and Isabella was not enough anymore. At first, it was wonderful; there's nothing else like it. Troy told me that I would be able to travel outside my body and join with different angels and not get bored with just one. It was such a rush of excitement and satisfaction, and even Isabella looked so beautiful and stronger. And afterward, it was like they relaxed all my muscles, and I was in a deep trance. And for the first time, I felt like I was being lifted out of my body and moving around with them. I could see myself looking so peaceful from the ceiling. The angels promised me that they would never hurt me or leave me, and Troy was giving me these drugs for a year.

"But then I could not get enough of them, and I wanted more and more. The more I wanted to hit my peak of pleasure, the more I couldn't. Troy told me I was burned out and old, and these drugs wouldn't work for me anymore. I thought he loved me. So now I am on hard drugs just to cope. I just started using syringes to speed up my fix.

"I didn't realize how powerful these demons could get until we all met at the agency, and I was frightened when I saw you had all that power. That's why I pretended to go away this weekend. I wanted to stop doing drugs and get away from those dark angels. But I couldn't do it on my own; it was too hard. That's why I went to Troy this weekend to beg him for one more hit. I would do anything for it, Charles, even betraying you to Merit and Beelzebul. Why did you want to help me? I thought you were in his power. I can never look you in the eye now; I am so ashamed of myself."

Charles calmed her down and started to tell her about what has happened to him.

"Sally, Suba left me alone a few days ago. He fought a battle at the agency, and he lost. Thank God I asked God for forgiveness, and I gave myself to God. I promised to serve Him. Now I have true peace that I have never had before. You remember my friend Tobit? He has been praying for me for many years."

Sally interrupted him. "Tobit? Didn't he die many years ago? How do you know he was praying for you?"

Charles answered. "I have seen his…" He paused for a moment, making sure he would not unveil Sarah's secret. "…sister-in-law, Jean. It is a long story, Sally. There are angels all around us fighting for our freedom, and Tobit is one of them. He appeared to me, and I have seen the other angels who have helped me so much. Now, I have Jesus Christ and his Holy Spirit—the true Spirit of God, not the counterfeit spirit we had before. Please give yourself to the one God, and you will truly be at peace. I will take you now to the clinic, and you will get well with His help."

Gabriel walked into the room to intervene. "Charles, Sally can't see me. She will have to go through rehab. She will need the time to heal on her own. Sally will listen to you, but she will go on her own journey. And she will help many others kick the habit too. And yes, Charles, she will come to know Jesus too, and she will be a powerful witness. Her husband Martin will take her back. He too has been praying for her. He has been a Christian for years now, and his prayers will soon be answered."

Sally agreed to go get the help she needed. Charles did not go into his relationship with Sarah. Sally knew that he was leaving her. Charles had enough money to send Sally to the best clinic where she could stay until she was off the drugs.

After taking her to the facility, he headed back to his apartment. Thomas then told Charles he will have to go to Sarah's hiding place. Charles had no idea where to go, so Gabriel told him to park his car at his apartment, and they will take him there because time was getting short.

Chapter 12

PRAYER WARRIORS

Michael appeared to Maria and Robert. "Do you remember going to your grandparents David and Casilda's cabin in Prince William Forest Park, Robert? They will contact you to see how you are doing because they could not come to see you. I want you and Maria to tell them you are coming to see them. This will be your excuse to leave the house. And your parents won't worry about both of you."

Robert replied, "You know, I did miss a call from them earlier. I feel so bad. I should have called them right back. But with all that was happening, I never did call them back. My parents did tell me that they were not able come and see me. I told my mom I would go to the cabin and see them as soon as I could leave the hospital. Michael, wouldn't it be dangerous for them if those fallen angels follow us there?"

Maria chimed in, "Oh yes, Michael, why do we have to put out Robert's sweet grandparents? They might be frightened if anything were to happen. You know, Casilda was like an angel herself, next to my grandmom of course. And David always treated me as his own granddaughter. Well, come to think of it, he had a few stories about a secret service he was into. Wow, Michael. Here is another question for you: did Robert's grandparents have something in common with mine?"

Michael gave them a slight smile. "Robert, I will answer your question first. No, they will not be in any danger, and they will not be put out. They are expecting you. And yes, Maria, they have everything in common. Give them a call now and tell them you both are heading over tonight. Oh, and tell them Michael sent you."

David and Casilda were more of prayer warriors than physical warriors. They were both from Portugal and had a great devotion to the Angel of Portugal who appeared to the children of Fatima in 1916 and also to Our Lady of Fatima who appeared to the children in 1917.

Now, our country needs the angels of God more than ever.

Tobit and Sarah depended on their powerful prayers. One of the most powerful prayers comes from the daily masses and saying the rosary. The power of prayer can move mountains. And Maria and Robert would need their prayers as they made the trip to Robert's grandparents' cabin because Beelzebul will throw whatever he could to stop them and retrieve the box before they get there.

Michael gave Maria and Robert new information. "Go to the lake at the back of the property. A row boat will be tied at the dock. Row to the center of the lake. The dark angels will be watching you, but that is what we want them to do. There, you will find an orange buoy with a chain attached to it. Pull on it, and you will find an identical box—the one we have to return to its proper place. It will be a decoy to distract Satan and his demons."

Maria became confused. "Why a decoy? Who has the real one?"

"Sarah and Charles will bring the real box to its destination. And your grandfather Tobit will guide it up to its new place, and he will be the guardian once it is back where it belongs."

"Michael, I wish I knew more about this Charles character. I don't want my grandmom getting hurt," Maria said with concern in her voice.

Michael assured her that everything was going to work out well and reminded her to trust in God.

"I have to leave you now. I must go and prepare Sarah and Charles for their mission and also to assign commanders to train our recruits to defend us in battle. Remember, Sam will be guarding you, Robert. But you must not let your guard down. The evil one will tempt you with everything he can. Don't hesitate to call on Sam for help."

*****

Charles finally met up with Sarah. She was so worried he would not make it back in time.

"Charles, I have been praying for your safety from the enemy. I was told you would be tested; now that you are here, I assume you have passed. And Sally, how did she take the news about us?"

Charles told Sarah about the horrifying events. He ensured her that Sally will be fine, and even though Sally and Charles have separated, he did not tell her about Sarah.

Sarah understood after she heard about what had happened. Charles took her hand, and they both began to pray for strength and guidance for what was to come.

Gabriel came into the room while Sarah and Charles were praying. Heather and Linda, along with their angels, were outside keeping guard until Michael gave the orders to lead Sarah and Charles to their destination.

Finally, Michael appeared in the room. "Sarah, I want you to go to the house and pack an overnight bag. You and Charles will be going to a cabin near Powell Creek. Bring your fishing rods so it looks like you and Charles are going on a fishing trip. The evil spirits are focusing on Maria and Robert right now. But Beelzebul is still keeping watch over Charles because he lost the battle for his soul, so he might have some dark angels watching what Charles is up to and trying to find a weakness so they can trip him up and get him back into their loop. Be on guard, both of you. Sarah, you know they think you are Jean, so play the part. They would also like to get Jean back after what had happened to Bella. They plan on getting a two for the price of one. Keep in constant prayer to invoke the Holy Spirit; He will keep you from temptation. Tomorrow morning, Heather and Linda will guide you to the place where an unexpected tornado will come down on the Marine Corps base. You will not be harmed or seen by anyone. I must go now. God be with you in Jesus's name."

Sarah wanted to ask so many questions, but Michael vanished in front of their eyes.

She turned to Charles. "Okay, let's go to my house… Oh, I am going to have to play my part… Let's go to Sarah's estate, and I will pack my bag for our fishing trip tomorrow."

Charles replied, "Yes, Jean, let's go and do His will and make Him proud of his new soldiers."

Sarah first went to get the box in her secret place. Charles was seeing the box for the first time. He went to reach for it, and Sarah began to have a flashback of Jean almost being taken by Bella.

She stopped Charles, telling him, "You can't open the box. It must be closed at all times."

"What will happen if we open it? No one really explained to me what the purpose of the box is."

Sarah sat down and tried to explain it the best way she could. "Well, I will try to shed some light on the question. You know we all feel some guilt after we sin against someone we love. So we go to God for forgiveness, and if we are sincere, God takes our guilt away. You remember in catechism class, we were taught that our lives were recorded in a book, and on Judgment Day, it will be read back to us. But God promised to wipe our sins from the books if we are truly sorry and repent.

"I admit I don't know all the answers regarding its purpose. Only God will reveal it at the proper time. What I do know is that if the enemy gets their hands on it, they will use it to spread the guilt of sinners, and they will feel hopeless. A hopeless country will believe the lies of those against our country's constitution. Our country will not be 'We the People' anymore; it would be 'We your Government and we know what is best for the People'."

Charles looked into Sarah's eyes. "Why would God have me involved in something of great importance? I am the last person God could have called. I almost betrayed you and your whole mission."

Sarah just smiled. "You know, that was exactly how Saint Paul felt. And if it wasn't for God giving him a chance, we gentiles would not have found out that we too can have salvation through God's son, Jesus. He wanted to arrest and kill Christians. But God used him as He is using you now. Instead of feeling unworthy, you need to be proud to be a child of God."

With that answer, Charles understood. He and Sarah proceeded to get what they needed from Sarah's house to go to the cabin near Powell Greek.

*****

Robert finally got through to his grandfather.

"Hello, Robert. I have been waiting for your call. How are you feeling? I have been so worried," David said.

Robert replied, "I am doing very well, Gramps. Your prayers have had a real effect on my recovery; I am sure of that. You know why? A good friend of mine suggested I come for a visit to see you and grandma. He told me to tell you Michael send me."

There was a moment of silence on the phone. Then David spoke, "Really, Robert? You are now working with the Secret Service of Angels! Is Maria with you too? Your grandma and I have been prayer warriors for her grandparents. Please come right away; we have your old room here for you. And Maria is welcome too. She can stay in our guest room."

Robert's gramps was on speaker, and Maria chimed in. "Yes, Grandpa David, I am with Robert. We need you and Casilda's prayers. We will be over in about an hour. Thank you for making us feel so welcome."

Robert switched off the speaker and told his gramps he loved him and will see him soon.

"Let's go before our parents get back. What about the agency in Quantico? Michael told us they are somehow involved in helping us."

Just then, there was a knock on the door. Maria looked at Robert, wondering who it could be. It was the three agents: Daymin, Nathan, and Nighjal.

Maria opened the door and let them in. "We were just on our way to Robert's grandparents' house. Michael said you guys are helping us, but we are not sure what it is we are doing. All we know is that we are decoys."

"Decoys!" The three men exclaimed in unison.

Robert began to tell them what Michael told them about how Tobit would be the one to return the box and also be its new keeper once the box has been returned. He was not sure if they knew about Sarah yet.

Then Gabriel appeared. "Hello, everyone. Nighjal, did you bring all your camping gear with you?"

Daymin replied, "Camping! Nighjal, did you forget to tell Nathan and me something?"

Gabriel intervened. "Well, I did tell Nighjal he was going on a camping trip. I assumed he told you all. The Figueiredos own enough land so when Maria and Robert visit, you gents will camp out to keep an eye on things. We know the evil one will have his dark angels following you to get the box to give it to Beelzebul. Go now and Godspeed."

Chapter 13

Deceiver in Disguise

As soon as Gabriel left, a small group of dark angels appeared led by a new dark angel in command named Rubin.

"We know Maria and Robert are going to take the box to its proper place. Try and get as close as you can to get any clues. We have a spy disguised as one of their friends. He will let us know who has the box, and he will try to get his hands on it."

Meanwhile, back in the house, Maria, Robert, and their three companions were in deep prayer for protection and guidance.

Michael appeared to give them a clear picture of how important it was to keep this secret, even from each other. They could not even discuss it with each other.

He said, "Even though this is a decoy, this box is still necessary for Judgment Day. If you are truly repentant and your book is stored in this box, when it is open, your pages will be blank, but it will be filled with all your good deeds. Go ahead and open it, Maria, and tell me how you feel."

Maria began to have flashbacks of what happened the last time she touched the box. She glanced at the doorway and saw what looked like the Archangel Michael motioning with his head not to open it. She was frightened and looked at Michael. "Are you really Michael, or a demon disguised as Michael?"

"Why would you ask that, Maria? Whoever you are seeing at the doorway, have him come forward!" Michael commanded.

It was then Maria knew the difference between them.

Michael whispered in Maria's ear without saying a word. "Pretend you believe him so he will come in closer."

Maria refused to open the box. The impostor was confident and walked through the door.

Michael whispered again. "He won't come near me, so walk closer to him as though you completely trust him. Don't be frightened. He can't harm you, but he cannot get away because he will tell the other you have the wrong box. I will fade away, but I will still be here."

Everyone in the room could also hear Michael's orders. Maria began to walk to the doorway.

With a grateful voice, she said, "Oh, thank you, Michael. You saved me from that dark angel. Please come in, and I will pay you homage."

The dark angel glowed with pride and elation—the things that evil feeds on. "You do me homage, little Maria, and I will give you what you wish for and more."

In a split second, Maria was drawn away from the group and into the arms of the dark angel. Something went wrong; he was supposed to come closer to her, but he tricked her to do the opposite. He began to demand that she give him her soul so they could become one.

She spoke to him softly, "Come back into the room with me, Michael, and all my friends will give you homage too."

Now, he felt confident that she thought he was Michael. Then he thought it would make him more powerful if he had more followers and by giving the box to Beelzebul would move him up in rank.

Robert, not knowing where Maria was, began to panic. Michael assured him that He was in control of what was happening.

Maria came back in the room, and the deceiver came in from the doorway. He was still pretending to be Michael. Everyone persuaded him to come closer to the center of the group so they could kneel before him and give adoration. He headed toward the center of the prayer group and was as boastful as he could be. When he got there, the Archangel Michael also appeared looking at the demon in a commanding manner. The demon's true form was revealed with his red eyes as he tried to look for Maria, but Michael spread his wings, and he was unable to see anyone, only the fury in Michael's blue eyes.

"You will not return to your master, lowly one. I will send you to your eternal punishment in fiery Gehenna."

His mouth was shut tight so the others could not hear his screams. Down he went in an amber puff of smoke.

"I am sorry to put you through that, Maria. But I am proud of you. You trusted me with your life, and I trust you to lead and complete this mission. Now that we are all together, will you trust me now and open the container? Alexander and his company are watching over the house so no demons can enter."

Maria became calm and was not even hesitant to do what Michael told her to do. She looked around at Robert, Nighjal, Nathan, and Daymin as if to let them know it was okay, and she would not be harmed in anyway by touching what was in the box.

"I believe Michael, and that I can trust whatever he tells me to do. I will open the box, and if you'll let me, also have my good friends here with me now to lay their hands on it as well."

Michael agreed to her wishes.

Maria took the lid off the box; it appeared to be a small book, but their pages were empty. She told everyone to make a circle, and they all touched the book at the same time. But instead of guilty flashbacks, they experienced all the goodness in their lives.

Maria and Robert were together at one point, but it wasn't anything they could remember in their past lives. They both saw a little child growing before their eyes. It was a little girl asking both of them to come for her.

She quickly took her hand off the book and broke the circle. "I'm sorry, everyone. That was a better experience, touching that box. Did you all have your own vision of your past without any of the stupid mistakes we had made?"

She looked at Robert because she knew she had not finished telling him what happened after they last saw each other in the hidden room. She told him she had to tell him something, but he vanished and returned to his body in the hospital room.

Robert didn't mention that he was with her in their vision together. He didn't understand it, and he could feel that Maria wasn't ready to share it right now.

Daymin said, "I was with my grandparents and with Nighjal and Nathan. You remember, guys? Just before I went into the Marine Corps, we went to the mountains with Poppop and Mommom because they wanted us together before I left. That was one of our best times together."

Nathan and Nighjal agreed.

Robert then reminded everyone that it was time to go; they can reminisce on the way.

Maria put the box in a bag and began to put her luggage in the car. The guys just grabbed a few snacks and some bottled water for the trip. Nighjal had all his camping gear in the car.

"I need a minute. You guys go to the car; I'll be right out," Nighjal told them while he made his pit stop.

*****

Sarah and Charles pulled up at the house just before everyone left. Maria ran out of the car to her grandmom and gave her a big hug. And she remembered her part.

"Jean, I was so worried when you didn't come home. We are headed up to Robert's grandparents' cabin. You have to fill me in on what is going on with you and Charles. What are you two doing here?"

Sarah replied, "We decided to go to Powell Creek for the weekend and do some fishing. I know Sarah has some fishing rods here. And I also need a change of clothing,"

Nighjal passed by Sarah. "Hi, Jean. Sorry, we can't stay and chat; we are camping on the Figueiredos' property. Take care."

Sarah went to Maria and Robert one more time and told them to be careful and wished them Godspeed. Then everyone went on their way.

Sarah and Charles went back into the house. They heard someone running down the stairs. "Who could that be? No one should be home," said Sarah.

"Let me go in first, Jean," Charles said in a concerned voice. He then spoke in a stern manner. "Who is there?"

The person answered, "It's me, Nighjal. I just had to use the bathroom before we left. And who are you? Oh, Charles, what are you doing here, and where is everyone? Why would they leave me here? I'm the one driving."

Sarah was frantic. "Oh, my Lord, Nighjal, your friends are in grave danger. A demon disguised as you took them to the Figueiredos' cabin."

Nighjal knew he had to act quickly. He couldn't call his friends because the impostor would suspect something was up.

"Jean, please call Maria and tell her what has happened. If she calls Daymin, she can tell him what is going on. And tell her to tell him not to talk at all about why they are going. I will have to find a way to get there myself."

Charles spoke, "We have to get you out of here so the other demons don't see you leaving. Wait a minute, Jean, didn't Michael say Heather and Linda's angels were going to travel with us?"

Charles had to keep using Jean's name just in case the enemy was listening in.

"Yes, Charles, I will ask for their assistance. Nighjal, when they come, they will guide you to my car. It is parked near the other house on this property." Then she began to pray. "Please appear to us, angels of God, and help our friend not to be seen by the dark angels."

Heather appeared immediately. "I'm here, Sarah. And our angels are ready to protect Nighjal. Nighjal, we will guide you to Sarah's car. Sarah, please don't be worried. You have to remain calm. You and Charles must act like lovers going on a holiday together. Beelzebul must not find out what you are up to. You can call Maria and tell her what is going on. My company of angels will keep watch."

Nighjal was ready to leave. Linda and some of her angels made sure to conceal him and get him safely to Sarah's car.

Sarah called her granddaughter.

"Hello, Jean. What is wrong?" Maria asked.

Sarah whispered on the phone. "I have some bad news. Nighjal is not driving with Daymin and Nathan. It is a demon disguised as Nighjal. You must call them and warn them not to speak to each other about the mission. Nighjal is driving to the cabin now in my car. If there is any way they can persuade the impostor to stop somewhere, maybe Michael will be able to intervene."

Maria hung up and immediately called Daymin.

Daymin heard his phone ring. "Hi Maria, what's up?"

"Daymin, pretend to laugh because I just told you something funny I saw while driving."

Daymin began to laugh. "Oh, really? I missed that. You want to know if we have David and Casilda's address on our GPS? Yes, we have it."

Maria's voice was a little bit lower now. "Nighjal is not driving the car. It is demon disguised as him. Make some excuse to stop at the nearest store. I am going to contact Michael to come to your rescue. Don't talk about our mission in the car. Do you think I can text Nathan without the driver suspecting anything?

Daymin said, "Yes, it's too bad Michell couldn't make it. But I know she will contact him soon. Maybe we can meet at the convenience store about a mile or two down the road. You know, just to pick up a few things, especially coffee to keep us awake."

"Okay, Daymin. Thanks."

Maria began to text Nathan.

> Pretend I am Michell. Your driver isn't Nighjal. He is a demon. Just play along with Daymin.

Nathan said, "Yeah, Daymin. Speaking of the little angel, Michell just texted me. She was wondering why I didn't text her yet. She couldn't call because she was at a meeting."

"Why don't we turn on the radio? I think Nighjal has it set on the EWTN talk show," said Daymin, knowing darn well a demon would shiver at the mention of Jesus's name.

"Nighjal" replies, "I think some music would be better to keep us awake for the long drive." He changed the channel to the oldies.

"That's Poppops' channel, Nighjal. You remember?" Daymin was humoring Nighjal so he wouldn't suspect that they knew who he was.

*****

Nighjal finally made it to the car safely. He was now on his way to catch up with the guys. He spoke into his iPhone to text Daymin:

> Hope Maria texted you what is happening. I am on my way in Jean's car. Did you pass the spot we like to go to for snacks and fuel? Let me know, and I will meet you there. Try to stall him, and I'll call Maria to stop there too. Hopefully one of the archangels will help us. Take care.

He then called Maria, "Hello, Maria. It is Nighjal."

Maria was so glad he was okay. "Oh, Nighjal, I am so happy you are okay. I thought the demon would harm you. He must have known you would try and contact us. I hope the others did not see you leaving."

Nighjal replied, "No, Jean had special angels with concealing powers, and they led me to her car. I plan on meeting Daymin and Nathan at the service station we usually go to. Have you contacted Michael yet? We have to confront this demon and make sure it does not get back to its master."

Robert told Maria to put the phone on speaker so he could hear what Nighjal was saying and so he can talk too.

"We have not heard from Michael. But I feel like he has another option for us. Michael told me to call on Sam if I needed help. He has given him command of the guardian angels. Maria and I will pray for his help, and we'll meet you there. Let's not text the others yet because he might catch on."

"Will do. I should get there in about twenty minutes. Take care," Nighjal answered.

Maria and Robert finally pulled into the service station. They had a head start and were there before them. They parked in the back in case they would have an issue with the impostor.

Robert turned to Maria. "I think we had the same vision at the house. Was there a little girl asking us to come for her? Is that why you broke the circle so soon?"

She hesitated to answer, but she finally did. "I do have to tell you something. That night, at the college party… All these years, we didn't even know who we were with. I really can't say it wasn't our fault because we should not have been there in the first place. I almost wish I could remember being with you. I always wanted my first time to be special, with someone I loved. I did like you but not that way because I was young, and I thought of you as my best friend."

Robert interrupted. "And how about now? Do you still like me as a friend?"

"Robert, now you are much more than a friend. I love you, and I want to spend my life with you."

He put his arms around her. "I love you, Maria. I have always loved you. There is no one in my life right now because I also want to spend my whole life with you."

She began to tell him the rest of the story. "My parents took me to the hospital after the party, and it was confirmed that I was raped. I was so upset thinking that it happened to me. But when you told me what happened to you, I realized you would never have raped me. You were on ecstasy pills, just like I was. I could not make out who I was with."

Robert told Maria he felt the same way, except he thought she was the college girl.

"Well, a few months after, I found out I was pregnant. I was so frightened to tell my parents but I had to. That was why they sent me away so no one would know I was having a child. I gave her up for adoption. It was the hardest thing I ever had to do."

She began to cry, and Robert held her close. "Don't feel bad. I love you, and I know our little girl is somewhere waiting for us. That is why we had the same vision. We will find her after this mission. Look! Daymin and Nathan are pulling up now. We need help soon. Let us pray for backup."

They held hands and prayed. "Oh dear, Lord Jesus, we need your help please. We were told by Michael to summon Sam and his company if we needed him, and we do now. Thank you, Lord, for hearing and answering our prayer."

"Hey, friend, I was told you could use my help."

Robert look over his shoulder. Instead of Sam, there was a gas attendant in overalls with grease on his face and hands from working on a car.

"My name is Sam. I own this station. At least for today, I do." He began to laugh. "How do you like my disguise? The enemy is not the only one who can change their appearance."

"Wow, you sure fooled us!" Exclaimed Maria.

*****

Before the guys got out of the car, the impostor questioned, "Maria and Robert do have that box with them, don't they? We should ask them if we can hold on to it just in case you-know-who is watching them. You know, no one would think we would have it. What do you think about that, Nathan? Why should we let those younger ones get all the credit? You have more years on them. I'm going to go over there now and talk to them about this."

Nathan said, "Look, Nighjal, just calm down. I'm going to get some gas, and Daymin is going in for some coffee and food. We'll talk about it later. We are just going camping, remember? Let's just keep it at that for now."

"Fine, Nathan, keep pretending all you want. But I am going over to them now."

They all got out of the car.

Daymin went to walk with his "cousin." "Hey, Nighjal, wait up! I will go with you. You know, I was wondering why these younger Marines are taking over too. What makes them better than us?"

Of course, Daymin didn't mean anything he said. But he was just stalling until help arrived.

Then the demon put his arms around Daymin and led him to the back of the station where Maria and Robert were. He pushed Daymin into the men's room and had him in a chokehold. He took a roll of duct tape out of his pocket and taped his mouth shut then his hands.

"Thought you could fool me, Daymin? Look next to you; does he look familiar? Yesss, I am a demon, and here is your twin, my dear Daymin, ready and more evil than me to take your place."

The new impostor punched Daymin and knocked him out cold. "Come on, get his phone off of him and his wallet. Let's not mess this one up like you did at the house. You should have gotten rid of the other one so he couldn't follow us and warn them. Maybe we should kill him now like you should have done to the other Nighjal."

This demon was quicker and more aggressive and ruthless in getting the job done. He also got pleasure from watching innocent people die.

"You keep an eye out because I am going to try to wake him so I can watch him struggle while I choke him to death. This way, I can feel more powerful to go after Maria. Oh, what a sweet little one; I am going to enjoy this job. Beelzebul might even promote me."

"Hey, you know, I'd like to see you kill him. No one is coming; just do it already."

Daymin awoke, and the demon started for his throat.

He began to feel pleasure in what he was about to do and looked into Daymin's eyes. "How does it feel knowing you are going to get the life choked out of you? I know it makes me feel wonderful, just wonderful!"

Daymin was not afraid to die. The demon began to try and kill Daymin; he pushed him down, sat on him, and began to strangle him.

*****

Nathan ran over to Maria and Robert. "Daymin didn't get here with the demon? I saw them both walking to you. Something is wrong. I think the demon knew that we were on to him. Daymin is in danger. Where is Michael? We might be too late!"

Robert looked at Sam. "I'm here, and Daymin is in trouble," the guardian angel said. "There are two demons trying to kill him in the rest room. Go, Nathan, our guardian angels will assist you. Now!"

Robert and Nathan both ran to Daymin's aid. But when they got there, they saw him standing there.

"Hey, guys. What's the problem? You both need the restroom that bad?"

"We were told you were in danger. And where is Nighjal?"

"He is in the restroom, as usual."

Sam appeared, but this time, he was in his full battle armor. He was hoping they were not too late.

"What have you done to Daymin, you impostor? I cast you down to burn in hell by the power given to me by God Himself," he commanded.

Nathan pushed the doors to the restroom open, and there was Daymin, laying on the floor.

Maria was left at the back of the store. She was about to go over to help, then she saw Nighjal.

"Is that really you, Nighjal?"

"Of course, it is, Maria. Is the box safe?"

Maria turned to go to the car when Nighjal put his hands over her mouth so she could not yell for help.

"Let's go. Get in the car. I will take the box after we get far enough. Then we can have some alone time together, just you and me. How does that sound? Oh, it's a shame you can't talk. Hurry, get in before they get back here." He hit Maria, pushed her inside the car, and sped off.

Nathan took off the duct tape and started CPR. "He will be okay. His angel kept him safe. The demon was getting no enjoyment because Daymin was not afraid of him. His double wanted to get to Robert and Maria before you came looking for Daymin."

"Oh no, Maria is alone!" Robert began to run, but it was too late. He was almost hit by their car as the demon drove by them. "Sam, what is happening? I thought you could stop this. Help me, Sam! Maria is all that matters to me now. Please, Sam, tell me she will be okay!"

Sam told him, "She will be, Robert, I promise. We have to keep a clear head now, and don't panic. You always told me to trust in God. Now is my turn to tell you the same."

Just then, the real Nighjal drove into the lot.

Sam began to issue order. "Nighjal, you take Daymin to the cabin. He will tell you what just happened. I don't have time to explain. The demon took Maria, and Robert and I are going after them, Godspeed."

Sam and Robert quickly got into the car. They were sure he was headed for the cabin.

*****

"This is going to be my finest hour. I am going to pull over at the next dirt road and hid out there, and when Maria comes to, she will give me the box. I'll park right here; no one will find us in this isolated road. Well, I hit her a little too hard. I guess I can start to search Maria before she wakes up."

As soon as Maria woke up, she asked, "What do you think you are doing?" She looked at his face, and it was not Nighjal's anymore.

"I want that box, Maria. I am looking for it." The dark angel put duct tape from his pocket and put it over her mouth. He knew that if she said His name, that would make him shiver and become weaker. Then he also taped her hands and feet. He pushed her out of the car and began to tie her to a tree.

Suddenly, she began to see other demons appear around the area and even next to her.

"You frightened? You should be because when we are done with you, you just might become one of us. When we find this box of yours, we will make you touch it, and your guilt from your sinful self on that night as a teen will play over and over again until you beg us to take it away and become one of us."

He began searching the car while the others tortured Maria with hopeless thoughts and fearful feelings. They told her about how Satan could give her anything her flesh desires if she just worshiped him instead of God.

One said to her, "Where is your God now, Maria? He doesn't care for you; he never did. Look at what he made you go through as a teenager. He even took your child away from you. Now look at you. If you don't give yourself to us, your Robert is going to die tonight trying to find you and your other friends."

Maria began to cry. They began to beat her until she became unconscious.

"Yesss, I found it! I found the box. Wake her up, you, fools. I want to enjoy seeing her face while she feels all the nasty things she has done that night."

Suddenly, there was a bright light, and what sounded like thunder surrounding the demons. It was Sam with his guardian angel warriors. And there was Robert running to rescue Maria with Nathan right behind him.

Sam was so massive in size and strength. He began to profess the name that would drag the demons to their knees in fear. The demons tried to flee, but most of them were vaporized. The one with the box almost got away, but Sam raised his sword which glowed so brightly the evil demon dropped the box and begged Sam for mercy. Sam was told to let this one go because then Beelzebul would think he was on the right trail; this way, Sarah and Charles would be successful in their mission.

Robert reached Maria and began to take the tape off her mouth and hands. "Maria, Maria!" He looked for Nathan. "Come here and help me with Maria!"

Sam spoke up, "Maria is okay, guys."

Robert looked at Sam, confused. "What do you mean she is okay? Look at her; she can't even get up."

Sam smiled and said, "Look again, Robert. Who do you see?"

They looked back at Maria. "What? Who is that, and where is Maria?"

"She is one of our angels disguised as Maria. I am sorry I couldn't tell you sooner. But we had to make it seem as real as it could be. Maria is safe. She is traveling with Daymin and Nighjal to the cabin."

Nathan interrupted, "We told Nighjal and Daymin to leave before we left."

Sam smiled. "You know Nighjal and his pit stops. When he went to the restroom, Maria ran to the car. She saw herself, but she was shielded from the impostor. But she witnessed everything that happened. When the demon sped away in the car, and Robert went after them with Nathan, then she ran to the car with Daymin. She told him about what happened. They were instructed to go the cabin and wait for you to arrive."

They were all relieved. "Good job, Sam, I am sorry I was upset back there. I guess I have to be more patient and trust that God is in control."

Sam understood. "Go now, and Godspeed. We will be keeping an eye on you."

With that, he and the others vanished before their eyes.

Maria, Nighjal, and Daymin arrived at David and Casilda's place safe and sound. Casilda had some good home cooking going on in the kitchen. It was a lot better than all the fast food they had been eating on the way there.

"Hey, guys, why don't you clean up before dinner? We have two bathrooms and a shower in the basement," David said.

He knew they needed it. As David had prayed for their safe arrival earlier, he had a few visions of what was going on at the service station.

As Daymin and Nighjal went to clean up for dinner, David stopped Maria.

"I know you had a close call back there. And I am very happy for you and my Robert."

She gave him a puzzled look. "How did you know?"

"Casilda and I live a life of prayer. We also have visions from time to time. Robert and Nathan should be here soon. You refresh yourself, and we will talk more when they arrive."

Robert and Nathan finally arrived. Casilda opened the door; she was so happy to see her grandson.

"Robert, it's been so long. You look well. I was so worried about you! Hello, Nathan. Thank you for taking care of my Robert. Everyone is getting ready for dinner. Both of you wash up before we eat. Then we can do some catching up."

Finally, everyone sat at the dinner table. It was time to chill and relax before their mission tomorrow.

Chapter 14

YOU CAN'T JUDGE WHAT'S IN THE BOX BY ITS COVER

Sarah and Charles just reached the Powell Creek cabins. Before entering the park itself, they parked the car and went into the office to check in.

A stranger walked up to Charles. "Hi there! Have you come up here for the fishing, or is this your honeymoon?"

"We are here for the fishing for now and some needed relaxation," Charles replied.

"This is my first time here. A good friend told me about it. In fact, I was stood up on this trip. Maybe I'll see you tomorrow if you both get up early," the stranger said.

Sarah was checking in while Charles was talking to the stranger.

"Okay, Charles, we have cabin 26. It's right on the lake, great for fishing."

"Great, Jean, let's go." Charles was still keeping the charade up.

When they left for their car, the stranger asked the front desk if cabin 25 was available.

"Who was that guy?"

Charles answered, "I'm not sure. But for some reason, I don't trust him."

They found their cabin and began to bring their luggage and fishing gear in.

"Look, isn't that the stranger we saw at the office? I hope he doesn't interfere with our visit here," said Sarah.

Charles replied, "He looks familiar but vaguely. You know, he asked me if we were on our honeymoon. I really wish we were." He then took Sarah in his arms and whispered in her ear, "I want so much to call you Sarah."

She whispered back, "So do I, Charles. So do I."

The stranger did know Charles. Charles did see him before, but he never met him. He had been stalking Charles since the meeting they had at the agency. Why was he here now? Sarah and Charles had to get this mission completed before this weekend ends. They cannot afford more obstacles getting in their way.

"Sarah, I know I shouldn't say that, but how long do I have to call you Jean?" Charles was not thinking clearly.

"Please, Charles, we are not always protected by our angels. Look at me. We have to focus on our job and get it completed as soon as possible."

Charles agreed.

After taking their stuff out of the car, Sarah put her luggage in her room with Charles doing the same. They came together in the main room.

"Let's pray for strength to do what God has for us next. Look, there is a Bible; that is a weapon we can use." Sarah turned the pages to Psalm 27:1: "The Lord is my light and my salvation, whom should I fear? The Lord is my life's refuge; of whom should I be afraid?"

They both felt at peace.

After their prayers, Charles went back to the office for a few items and a guide map of the area.

The occupant of cabin 25 watched Charles leave the cabin. Now he had the opportunity to visit cabin 26. Waiting for Charles to be out of sight, he began to walk to Sarah's cabin.

Sarah was unpacking when she was startled by a knock on the door. "Who is there?"

"Jean? It is me, John Taylor. You might know my father, Nathan Taylor."

Sarah went to the door. "John! I haven't seen you since you were a young boy. What are you doing so far from home?"

John answered, "I don't want to be too long, Jean. I just stared working for the agency. I am the chaplain for the Marine Corps Base at Quantico. My dad never wanted me to get involved in his secret missions. But I have been in the secret service for about a month now. I was following you. I was spying on the satanic prayer group. I was trying to warn you about Charles. He was the leader of this satanic ritual. I thought he was after Maria, but when I saw you leaving with him. I had to see what he was up to. Why don't you leave now while he is at the office?"

Sarah was wondering why Nathan didn't tell him she was not in danger. "When did you last speak with your dad?"

John told her that he didn't tell his dad because he didn't want him to know he was in the group. He had wanted to tell him, but he was afraid of his reaction.

"John, you have to tell your dad. He would have told you everything is okay now."

Just then, Charles was back at the cabin and opened the door. "Sarah, I forgot my wallet."

John heard him say the wrong name; hopefully, no one else did.

"Who are you? What are you doing here? Jean…why did you let him in?"

"Sarah! Jean! Which one is it, Charles?"

Sarah intervened. "Charles, it is okay. This is John Taylor, Nathan's son. He is very new to the agency and thought he could do it on his own. Didn't you, John?"

"Sarah or Jean, whoever you are…wait, I remember Sarah and Tobit died in a lightning storm. I was not there when it happened, but I remember my parents telling me. The story was in the papers when I was doing research on some of the past missions," John said. "Look, I am sorry about this and for hearing what I shouldn't have heard. If it means anything, I am a priest, and I will not tell anyone our secret. My name is Father John."

"Well, Father John, we trust you. Don't call your dad now because this mission cannot reach the ears of the evil one," Sarah told him.

Charles joined in. "Yes, Father John, we can't tell you, but if you'd like, please pray for us."

Father John visited with Sarah and Charles for about two hours. He gave them his blessing and went back to his cabin.

As he was leaving, he said, "Nice meeting you, Jean and Charles. Maybe I will see you tomorrow, and we can catch a few fish together."

*****

Charles and Sarah were about to get their needed rest. So was Maria and Robert. Daymin, Nathan, and Nighjal had their campsite ready and were getting the rest they needed too. The next day would be challenging; even though they had two missions, their timing had to be identical.

While everyone was sleeping, the archangels, Sam, and his guardian angels, Alexander and his company and Heather and Linda and their company were preparing for battle to protect the humans. Michael was going over everyone's responsibilities in carrying out this complex and precisely timed mission; It had to come together perfectly.

He started giving commands on who was to go where. "Sam, you and your company will stay with me at Prince William Forest Park. Heather and Linda, you and you company will help Sarah and Charles at Powell Creek with Gabriel. Alexander, you and your company will be stationed at Marine Corps Base Quantico with Raphael. There is going to be a storm tomorrow at noon from Fredericksburg to Powell Creek which will include Prince William Forest Park to Marine Corps Quantico and the Potomac River. Our enemy will be in full force trying to get the other box. They will think they are victorious. This battle will be furious and will last for around three hours, so everyone needs to be on their best game. And we all know that we will carry out this mission in victory. Are there any questions?"

"Yes, Michael, I do. Are they all informed of what to do and how important their timing is? Last time I spoke with Robert, they were not told anything," Sam asked Michael.

"Sam, while they sleep, they will all have the same dream or, should I say, the same vision with instructions that are slightly different. One box will go up to the heavens, and Tobit will be the keeper. He will also be with Sarah and Charles. The other box will be placed at the bottom of the Potomac River next to MCB Quantico. At least, that is what the enemy will think. Father John Taylor will also have a dream, and he will help Maria and Robert get their box in the Potomac River, which will be only temporary."

Sam was going to ask another question about who Father John was but he didn't.

"Sam, I know you have many questions. You keep Maria and Robert safe. And when this all comes together, you will understand and know who Father John is and why he will be involved." Michael knew what Sam was thinking.

*****

Now Beelzebul had his own plan to go over with his most powerful demons. He had his own archdemons, and he was giving them their instructions. Astaroth, one of the archdemons, and his company of dark angels were placed near the Figueiredos' estate. Leviathan, a demon of the sea, was one of the few who can go into the water. Beelzebul knew he had to post him near the Potomac River. Leviathan had his dark angels on the bank of the river. Even though the demons did not suspect Charles and "Jean" of having the box, Beelzebul had Vapula, the dark angel of philosophy, and Merit, the one dark angel who wanted Charles when he was trying to help Sally, stationed with their small army at Powell Creek. He wanted to tempt Charles to lead his dark angels again. And he also called on Belial to entice Jean with his most beautiful dark angel.

"Listen up, everyone. This time, we will succeed in getting that box from Maria and Robert; they are sleeping now. And David and Casilda will be sleeping, and we don't have to worry about them praying. We will get into some of their dreams or what they think are their dreams."

When the demons arrived, they knew this had to be where the box was because there were so many angels guarding the cabin of David and Casilda. Even though the demons thought David and Casilda would be asleep, they were not. They actually took turns resting. So when one slept, the other was up in deep prayer. They knew how important prayer was for Maria and Robert to be successful in their mission.

Astaroth began to speak to his company. "We must make ourselves hidden until I give the word to attack. It will be near the river because that is where the box will be taken; we are sure of it. No need to stir up the guardian angels and their commanders."

The evil ones knew they could not defeat the act of the prayer warriors. They only prey on human weaknesses.

*****

Weakness was what Vapula depended on with Charles. Vapula and Merit arrived quietly at cabin 26 while Charles and Sarah were sleeping.

Even though Sarah and Charles was protected by Heather and Linda's angels, God allowed some dark angels to test Charles and Sarah.

"Look, Merit, your host is in deep sleep. This is our time to try and enter his dreams. Bring him back to the night our leader gave him his spirit. We have to remind him of how good he felt when he had Suba as his dark angel. You stay in his bed until I persuade him to let you in. And Belial will go into Jean's room and remind her of what she would have if she let Bella have her. Belial is one of the most beautiful male angels there were. He will enter her dreams, tempting her to commit sin with Charles. Sin makes us weak, and weakness is just what I need. Charles will also have thoughts of his own about Jean."

Thomas and Pamela were there with Charles and Sarah, and they were in prayer for their safety. Pamela knew they would need more guardian angels in the cabin. Pamela stayed with Sarah and witnessed what Belial, the dark angel, was whispering in Jean's ear. He was reminding Sarah of what she was missing by not sleeping with Charles. He went into great detail about the pleasures she could have with Charles. He was so close to Sarah; she could feel him trying to caress her.

He whispered again, "Come on, Jean. You know you can't resist my temptation; no one can. I am the best at what I do. My master knows it; that's why I am here, to let you know what you are missing. My record for tempting you, humans, is off the charts. Come on, Jean, wake up and visit Charles in his room. He is eagerly waiting for your touch."

Vapula was in Charles's room with Merit. Angel Thomas also called for backup from other guardian angels.

Vapula began to whisper into Charles's ear while he was sleeping. "Charles, you are back at the agency, giving praise and worship to Beelzebul. He is giving you the gift of being in charge of the worshipers around you. Yes, Charles, you've never felt such power and excitement in your life. You know you want that feeling again, Charles. Relive that night now. Jean is going to come into your room soon. Merit is here waiting for his perfect host to celebrate with Jean and her dark angel Belial. You will also remember what it was like with Sally. Jean's angel, Belial, is much stronger than Isabella."

Charles's dreams were so real; he was actually having a vivid flashback. And he was enjoying every minute because, at that time, he did not know Jesus. He was talking in his sleep saying Sally's name and reliving that moment they had and couldn't imagine that feeling being any better. He was getting anxious to be with Jean and Belial.

He then relived his time at the agency. He could actually feel the same power he had. When will Thomas and Pamela stop this from happening?

Sarah was walking in her sleep and headed for Charles's room. She opens his door and Belial was right by her side. Merit was so excited to enter his new host. Sarah lay next to Charles in his bed.

"I will have victory again!" cried Belial. "Charles, go ahead and be with the one you love; she is ready for your caress."

He also whispered into Charles's ear all the things he told Jean. After listening to Belial, Charles was ready to let Merit come in as well.

But just when Belial and Merit were about to touch Charles and Sarah, a bright light from the angels filled the room. Pamela covered Sarah up with her robe, and Thomas called Charles's name.

"Charles, you are a child of God now. Remember, Charles, this was all in the past."

Charles suddenly had another flashback. But this time, he was with Sarah, praying for forgiveness and receiving the true Holy Spirit. At the same time, Pamela was showing Sarah her time with Charles when they were praying.

"No! We almost had them both in our hands. Why are you here? We will fight you all. We cannot stop our mission. Belial and I are Beelzebul's strongest dark angels. You saw how easy it was to entice these humans. You know you want to join us. Your God never told you that you can be your own gods. Just worship Beelzebul, and he will truly set you free to do whatever you want to. You can have these humans too." Vapula tried to convince some of the guardian angels from Heather and Linda's company to be on his side.

Instead, they led Sarah and Charles safety out of the room.

Belial said, "Where did Jean and Charles go? It is time to raise our swords and begin the battle for our humans!"

Sarah started to awaken, and so did Charles. "What are we doing here? I was having a strange dream. It was like I was watching myself doing something I didn't want to do, but I couldn't stop myself."

"Me too. I saw myself back in the past. I could not stop myself from reliving it," Charles said in a frightened voice. He realized Beelzebul's dark angel were in his bedroom, and he turned to Sarah and said, "Jean, I am sorry for having those feeling for you. I was supposed to protect you, and I almost led you into temptation. Please forgive me."

The angels then guided them to safety and reminded them it was not their fault. They were told to pray while the battle went on in the other room.

Vapula and Belial led the guardian angels outside. They were hoping to alert their dark angels to help them in their battle. But Heather and Linda's company were too strong, and the cloaking angels would make it impossible for any of the dark angels to find them.

The evil ones were surrounded by a multitude of angels. They surrendered their swords. The Archangel Gabriel appeared, and the dark angels, as strong as they were, appeared to tremble with fear because they knew what was going to happen.

"Should I let you face Beelzebul with your shameful loss, or shall I give you your just punishment in hell?"

They were pleading for mercy.

"No mercy for your ungodly acts. Here is your punishment." They saw a fiery abyss awaiting them.

Pamela and Thomas calmed Sarah and Charles down. Gabriel appeared to them too.

He told them, "We are going to protect you. Here is a rosary for each of you. Go to your own bedrooms and pray. You will sleep with peace of mind. The spirit of God will give each of you visions of what will happen tomorrow. Be brave; there is nothing more to fear. God will not allow you to be tempted again."

Chapter 15

Visions Coming Together

In cabin 25, Father John had a vision in the night telling him to go back to MCB Quantico.

Gabriel appeared to him when he went back to his place on the base. He let him know everything that was going on with Maria, Robert, Sarah, and Charles's missions. He did not expect to become as involved as he was because he was new with the agency.

"Father John, I know you are new to the agency. But God has chosen you to place this box in the Potomac River. It is only a temporary place until the other box is secure with Tobit who will be the keeper until Judgment Day. When the evil one finds out they were after the wrong box, you will retrieve it, and the angels of the Lord will lift it up to the heavens."

*****

Maria and Robert's night was restful even though they had visions of what they were about to do. David had started making breakfast for everyone. Casilda had the last prayer station, so David wanted her to sleep in.

Maria was the first one to come to the kitchen table.

"Good morning, Maria, I hope you slept well. You know now what you must do and where to go? Casilda and I have been taking turns all night praying for your safety. The dark ones tried to come and tempt you to give them the box, but our prayer kept them away from you and Robert. They are still around here waiting for you to start your journey. The gentlemen camping outside are starting to get up and put their camping gear together. You and Robert will tell them what their part is in your mission because only you and him had visions of what would happen today."

Maria replied, "Yes, David, I did have visions. I was assured that if things go wrong, God will make it right and not to panic because God is in control of everything that happens."

Robert came downstairs to join everyone in the kitchen. "Good morning! I smell something good. But Grandma is not up yet. How good can breakfast be if Gramps cooked it?"

David replied, "Well, your grandma taught me how to cook. Give it a try, smarty pants."

One by one, they all are in for breakfast. And finally, Casilda came to the table.

"Oh, what a surprise, Gramps made breakfast."

"Yes, Grandma, and it is almost as good as yours." Robert laughed.

Now that breakfast was finished and all were present, it was time to discuss the job at hand.

Robert talked first, "Maria and I will be traveling to the church in Triangle for the twelve o'clock Mass. The three of you guys will take another car and meet us there. One o'clock is when a severe windstorm warning will be in effect."

Maria joined in. "Everyone in the church will be on their way home before the storm starts. Nathan, your son John will be involved. I am not sure to what extent. I did see him in my vision, but he was on the river. I am sorry; I don't know anything else. Robert, did you see him too?"

Nathan became very upset. "What? I told him not to ever get involved with this part of the agency! He is my only son! I won't be able to bear it if anything happened to him. It was hard enough when he was deployed as a chaplain in Afghanistan. But I know I have to trust God to protect him."

Robert said, "Yes, I did see Father John in my vision too. And, Nathan, he will be in the stormy river, but Jesus will be with him. You, Daymin, and Nighjal will accompany Alexander and his fallen heroes at MCB Quantico. You all have clearance to enter the base. Sam and his company will be with Maria and I."

Maria also let everyone know that their timing was very important.

*****

Beelzebul's troops of dark angels were keeping their eyes on every move Maria and Robert made.

"They have Sam and his angels guarding them. Sam is much stronger than before. We will still put up a fight to keep them from noticing Leviathan going to the Potomac River to capture the box before it hits the water. He is the only one here that can go in the water."

He wanted his dark angels to distract Sam and his angels.

One dark angel named Fearless spoke up, "Beelzebul, I will confront Sam and challenge him to fight me. You know I won't stand down for anyone, especially no new fallen hero. I'll show him what a real hero is about."

Beelzebul agreed; but if he loses, his name will be changed to Fearful.

"They are headed for the church. We cannot go in, but I think Sam and his angels will be outside watching out to see if we are coming."

That was exactly what was happening. Everyone arrived at church, and Sam was outside with his angels guarding the area.

Father John was the priest saying the Mass. Nathan was seated in front. He did not know his son was going to say the Mass. He could not hold back his tears knowing his only son would be in danger.

Nighjal asked him quietly, "Are you okay?"

Nathan didn't want anyone to know he was crying, so he replied, "Yes, all the flowers in here must be bringing out my allergies."

Daymin was on Nathan's other side. He whispered, "You know I'm the one with the allergies, bro. Don't worry, we won't let anything happen to John; he is a man of God. Now let God do His work."

Nathan felt encouraged by their concern and kind words of truth.

Father John was about to make his sermon. Then he noticed his father was sitting in the front row pew.

"Good afternoon, everyone, my name is Father John Taylor. I am a chaplain at MCB Quantico. I want to thank you for welcoming me to your beautiful church. Your pastor will be back next Sunday. My father is here today, and I am hoping my sermon will not put him to sleep."

The congregation began to feel more comfortable with this visiting priest and began to laugh at his small humor.

"Most of us would not easily give up on our children no matter how old they get. We want to keep them as safe as possible. I notice that even some of my parishioners' children are at an age when they can leave the nest, and their parents are reluctant to let go.

"Our reading today was about Abraham and his son Isaac. Abraham was really not so different from any other parent. But he had a relationship with God that most people don't have today. God asked him to do the unthinkable: to give up his son as a sacrifice even though God promised to make his descendants as countless as the stars in the sky. He completely trusted in the Lord to fulfill his promises. Without question, Abraham did as the Lord told him. Maybe somehow, Abraham knew that God would have stopped him. And He did just that when the angel of God blocked his dagger to prevent him from offering his son Isaac. How many times has God sent his angels to help us in our lives today? And how many of us would not even be at this church today if not for your guardian angel who guided us here?

"In our second reading, Paul gives us his very powerful word: 'If God is for us, who can be against us? He who did not spare his own Son for us all.' God was letting Abraham know that one day, God himself would give up his own Son, and Abraham did not have to give up Isaac.

"In our Gospel, Peter, James, and John, on a high mountain, witnessed Jesus being transfigured before their eyes with Elijah and Moses speaking to Jesus. God spoke to them these words: 'This is my beloved Son, listen to Him.' Once again, God is telling His disciples to trust Him no matter how impossible the situation may be. After Jesus's death and resurrection, the apostles finally knew what Jesus meant when he told them not to tell anyone until the Son of Man had risen from the dead.

"I don't want to keep you here too long because it looks like we are headed for a bad storm. Just one more thing, for my own father, trust God for whatever missions He has for me as well."

Everyone was finally on their way home after the Mass was over. The only ones left were Maria and Robert and the team of Secret Service of Angels ready to do whatever it takes to complete their mission.

They all began to have a moment of intense prayer and guidance from above. Father John led everyone in prayer. The Holy Spirit came upon them all to protect them from the evil spirits that will try to distract them from the job at hand.

Nathan was especially touched by the Spirit and began to speak to his friends but directed it at his son, John.

"Dearest, friends, we are here for only two reasons: to serve God and to serve our country. We are merely human, but God, in His infinite mercy, chose us all to accomplish our task to give our country the true freedom to choose good over evil. To my son, John, God has revealed to me that the gift he gave me twenty-five years ago will now be an instrument used by God today. So go with my blessing. My nest may be empty, but my heart is full of your presence."

Now, it was time for everyone to take their places. Nathan, Daymin, and Nighjal headed for the MCB Quantico but not before Nathan went in for one more hug from John. Daymin and Nighjal had to join in before they departed. Maria and Robert said their goodbyes as well.

The storm was indeed coming. The day that started out sunny and clear became cloudy and slightly windy. It was now one in the afternoon, and the sky grew ominously darker. Hundreds of dark angels led by Astaroth tried to surround Maria and Robert. But Michael and Sam had their own hundreds of angels surrounding them, so the dark forces could not penetrate enough to even whisper in their ears the lies that demons wanted to tell them.

Astaroth spoke in a thunderous voice, "Michael, are your humans so weak they need all that protection from us? Let's get this battle started so we can get some clearance and test these pathetic human creators."

Maria and Robert could not see all the angels around them. Finally, Michael appeared in front of them with Sam. Father John had not seen Saint Michael yet because he had to go back in the church to make sure everyone had gone home and that all the sacred articles were securely stored in their proper places.

Michael spoke to them, "Maria and Robert, you cannot see this battle that is about to begin. You must stand behind me, and do not listen to any whispers about stopping Father John from getting into the boat and taking the box into the Quantico Creek headed to the river. They will tell you they are going to harm him, and even though it may look like he won't make it, God is in control. That is why I sent Nathan to the Marine Corps base. I know he would try and rescue him. The demons are going to put up a relentless battle. You both will hold on to the box until you get near the boat and hand it over to Father John. Keep your focus on Sam and me. Father John's guardian angel will lead him where he is to go, and some of Sam's angels will be around him to keep him from harm."

Father John knelt in front of the altar to say a prayer just before he left. He had his eyes closed. Then he felt a hand on his shoulder. He thought it was Maria or Robert coming to tell him it was time to leave the church. But when he looked up, he saw a beautiful angel. It was the Archangel Gabriel.

"Father John, I was sent by God to make sure you are ready to do His will and carry out this difficult task. You will be given the box by Maria and Robert. You are to go into the boat provided at the Quantico Greek. You will then take the boat to the Potomac River near the Marine Corps base. There is only one demon who can go into the water, and he will go after you to get the box. Are you willing and ready to complete this mission?"

Father John replied, "Yes, Gabriel, I am ready to do God's will. I admit, I am a little frightened. Please lay your hands on me to be filled with the Spirit of God."

Gabriel touched him and said, "In the name of Jesus, give Father John, your humble servant, your Holy Spirit to do battle against the evil one. John, the Spirit of God is upon you now. Go, and your guardian angels will lead you. I must go now to Sarah and Charles. This will all be over soon. Once their box goes up to heaven, your box will go up too after you take victory from the demon of the sea."

*****

Sarah and Charles were getting ready to go to the camping site office. They were inquiring about renting a motor boat for their fishing trip at Powell Creek. When they got to the office, it was closed.

She looked at Charles. "There is a note on the door:

> There is a storm warning until 3:00. Please stay in your cabins until after 3:00.

"Charles, we have to be on this creek and head for the Potomac River. We both had the same visions of being on a boat. No one will rent us one with this storm coming. Look at the sky; it is starting to get dark already."

Charles responded, "We will go back to the cabin and get our gear ready. I know Gabriel will come to give us instructions and edification."

They went back to the cabin waiting to be visited by Gabriel. They held hands and began to pray to God for advice on how they will get on the river.

Finally, Gabriel did appear to them. "My children, God heard our prayers. Heather and Linda, along with their company of angels, will assist you both. Tobit will also be with you on the boat. The enemy will not be able to see them. Someone will be coming to your cabin. Go with him; he will be your guide for your fishing trip on Powell Creek. The storm will not get intense until you are on the Potomac River. Please be brave; both of you will not be harmed."

Chapter 16

Aligning God's Instruments for the Earth's Final Days

Moments after Gabriel left, there was a knock at the door. When Charles opened it, he saw the stranger Gabriel had foretold.

"Good afternoon, sir, I heard you needed a guide for a special fishing adventure. Just in case the weather gets too bad for us to return, the boat is big enough for carry-on luggage. Michael filled me in on your mission at hand. And Sarah, you might recognize the boat we're about to go on."

"Who are you, and how do you know my real name?"

He replied, "I told you, Michael told me everything. And Tobit and I were good friends in the Marines. Let's get going before they won't let us go on the boat because of the weather."

Charles grabbed all their fishing gear, and Sarah took the box and their carry-on luggage and headed toward the lake. Sarah was going to ask more questions, but time was of the essence.

The dark angels stationed at Powell Creek noticed Charles and Jean leaving the cabin with the stranger. But they did not see Vapula and Belial anywhere near them. They assumed they were engaging with their victims in the cabin and did not want to interfere. Even Merit was nowhere to be seen.

*****

One of them spoke up, "Something is not right. Vapula, Belial, and Merit were in the cabin all night with Charles and Jean. We would have received a notice from Vapula if their mission did not take place. And for sure, they would not have come out of the cabin alone. Get ready to draw your swords; we have to head out and tell our master."

Linda and her angels surrounded the dark angels with their wings stretched so wide their tips touched the others. They also had their swords raised for battle. Linda commanded the dark angels to surrender or prepare for battle. There was no surrendering from the evil ones.

The battle was fierce, and at least two of the dark angels managed to escape their damnation.

"Now is your time, evil spirits, to descend to your eternal punishment in hell! Quick, three of you guardian angels, go and retrieve the two missing fallen angels. They must not reach Maria and Robert. I will alert the Archangel Michael and Commander Sam."

Linda's thoughts reach the ears of Saint Michael and Sam. They expected this to happen. The archangel let Linda know that everything was going as planned and not to get discouraged. They just had to continue what they were doing. They also told the three angels not to pursue the escaping demons and to go back to Linda's company.

"Okay, everyone, we must continue our mission. Michael has everything under control. Pamela, summon the three angels I sent out to go after the two who escaped. After that, go to Sarah and Charles on the boat to keep them from any harm on the Potomac River," Linda commanded.

"Thank you, Linda, for giving me that privilege of serving under your wings. Will Heather and her company be blocking their view from the sky?"

Linda answered, "Yes, Pamela and Tobit will be with them as well. I know you are worried about Robert and Maria. They are in good hands."

"Thank you. I was worried because the major battle is going on there now."

*****

Maria was carrying the box. She could not see the battle, but she could hear whispers telling her she was weak, and if she goes through with this, her friend Father John will be tormented by demons before they finally kill him.

Robert was holding on to Maria as they both started walking toward the dock.

She stopped to face him. "Robert, we must not listen to the voices whispering around us. I am not sure if you can hear them. Don't let go of me; I need you to keep me focused."

He held on to her and assured her with his words. "Dearest Maria, I will never leave your side. We are in this together. Let's get to Father John so he can get to the river before the water becomes too rough for him to launch his boat. We must trust God and forge ahead. Our part is almost over, Maria. I can see him in the boat."

Just before Maria could hand the box over to Father John, a gray mist swirled around both of them.

They heard a voice saying, "You are both bringing Father John to his death, you fools. You will live with your guilt from your friend's fate. That is just what we want. We have a secret weapon that will destroy your plans."

Back on the road, about a mile away, the two demons that got away from the battle at Powell Creek thought they escaped their punishment.

"We will get a promotion for this information we have for our master. Look, I can see our master!" The dark angel took flight with his partner.

But they were detained by Sam's angels. "You looking for someone?"

The evil angels replied, "Yes, we know the truth about the boxes."

Sam also appeared on the scene. He was so bright; the two dark angels were almost blinded. Sam stood tall with his extremely strong physique in full armor.

"You really think you can get by me and my company of angels? Prepare to receive your eternal punishment!" With his sword raised, he pointed it to the ground below, and the dark angels were pulled into a flaming vortex leading into the bowels of hell.

Michael summoned Sam and his company to return to Maria and Robert. They needed all the protection they could get because Beelzebul would go after them with a vengeance once he realized what was happening.

Sam was back in an instant. "Here I am, Michael. I will never leave Robert's side until he is no longer in danger."

Michael assured Sam. "I know you won't. That was why you were chosen to be his special angel."

Maria and Robert finally reached the boat that Father John was on. Robert took the box from Maria, stepped aboard, and handed it to Father John.

"God has given you this important container. Be brave; we are here praying for your safety. When you arrive at the Potomac River, the sea demon will try to take possession of the box. Don't resist because when he reaches to grab it, he will get a surprise. Also, the storm will be very violent, but your father and your uncles Daymin and Nighjal will come to your rescue."

Father John said, "Thank you, Robert, and thank Maria for me too. I know I will need all your prayers. Gabriel visited me and sent the Holy Spirit upon me to give me the strength I need." He then whispered into Robert's ear something to tell Maria.

"Okay, Father, I will tell her. We will go to the Marine Corps base and wait for you to return, victorious from your battle." Robert disembarked, and Father John drifted off toward the Potomac River.

*****

Sarah and Charles boarded the stranger's boat. When Sarah stepped on board, it seemed so familiar to her.

"I remember being on this boat before with Tobit. You said you were his friend?"

He replied, "Yes, Sarah, I am. We will go down memory lane after you do what you must do."

Heather and Linda were also on board. Their guardian angels flew around them so the dark angels could not see them leave. The Archangel Gabriel kept an eye on them all.

Everything was going as planned.

The sky grew even darker. And as predicted, the storm approached. Will all who were out in the water have the faith they needed to keep from losing their courage?

*****

The enemy Beelzebul would not be deceived for long. He hadn't heard back from any of his dark angels on what was happening with Jean and Charles, especially Vapula and Belial.

"As soon as Father John gets to the river, keep an eye out for the box. Just when he holds it up to give glory to God, have Leviathan move in for the kill. The moment Leviathan leaps into the waters, the river will become untamable. I cannot wait to see Michael's face when we finally take possession of the guilt of all mankind! Once and for all, this nation will be under complete government takeover. Then I will take over the ones who govern."

*****

So far, the enemy was too blinded by the possibility of taking the people's freedom away he did not notice that Vapula and Belial weren't reporting back to him. Hopefully, he would not know until he realized that this box was untouchable for any demon.

The three o'clock hour was almost at hand. There were only thirty more minutes for everything to come together.

Sarah and Charles made it to the river, and so did Father John. Sarah held on to the container the box was in as they arrived at their destination.

"Where is Tobit? Michael said he would be here to bring this up to the heavens. Oh, Charles, I am sorry, but I miss him so much. This would be the last time I'll see him, and we are almost there."

The stranger driving the boat started to slow it down, and it gradually came to a stop.

"Sarah, I miss you too."

She turned to him. "Tobit! It's you! My dear, why didn't you tell me?"

Tobit replied, "My dearest Sarah, I couldn't because I had to hide my identity from the enemy. I am sorry for being away for so long. And Charles, please take good care of Sarah for me."

Charles chimed in. "I will, Tobit. And I want to thank you for all of the prayers you said for my salvation. Please keep praying for us both."

Tobit embraced them both. "I have to take the box now. The enemy is going to discover that they had been misled. They will look for both of you. The river is starting to get a little choppy because the sea demon is going after Father John. When he does and tries to touch the box, he will not be able to because it contains only the good of all mankind. He will be extremely angry. He will report to Beelzebul, and then he will realize who he should have been after. It will happen quickly, so head the boat toward the Marine Corps base. And don't worry about Father John; he will get rescued by his father and his uncles. I love you, Sarah. But I have to get on with the mission."

Sarah hugged him, knowing it would be the last time she would see him on earth.

Tobit stood at the bow of the boat with the box. Linda and her company were above the boat watching out for Leviathan. Heather and their angels were between Father John's boat and Sarah's to warn Linda when Leviathan was on his way.

*****

Father John was about to raise the box to heaven with this prayer on his lips: "Dearest Father, it is my privilege to present the good book on which is written every good deed that mankind has done because the death of your Son for our weakness made it possible to completely erase all our iniquities. I am prepared to face the storm knowing you have your arms around me to protect me from the demon of the sea. Thank you, Heavenly Father. Amen."

Leviathan immediately plunged into the river and headed straight toward Father John's boat. There were other demons flying above, cheering and discouraging Father John with insults and foul language, yelling at him, and calling him useless and unholy. They were letting him know that there was no hope for him, and he should kill himself because he has let everyone down.

Leviathan reached the boat as it was being tossed around the waters. Before he captured the box, he went to Father John telling him to toss himself into the river to commit suicide; this way, Leviathan will also have his soul as well as the box.

"When I get through with you, you will beg me to take your soul. I could easily take the box from you. But that is all what Beelzebul wants. I want to get some satisfaction as well. Put the box down and give me one moment of pleasure watching you suffer."

The box was blown out of his hands and onto the deck. Father John tried to grab it, but he couldn't. His body was bashed violently around the boat.

Leviathan held him up as though he were a rag doll. "Yes, Father, I can feel your pain. It is so wonderful. I wish I had more time to enjoy this feeling. Now, come on, kneel before me then dive off this boat and end it all, or I will torture you even more."

Father John was in unbearable pain; he could not even speak. He just wanted it to be over. Those few minutes felt like eternity. He began to crawl on his knees toward Leviathan as if he was going to worship him.

"Oh, yesss, John! Is it true? Could I have complete gratification from you worshiping me? That would give me such power, even more than Beelzebul's power! I promise you, you will not regret your decision. Please say the words I am yearning to hear: 'I long for your presence, Leviathan. Take all of me and my soul so I will not face this torture any longer.'"

The priest turned away from the sea demon and resisted the temptation to give his soul away. God gave him the strength to get the box. When he reached it, he tossed it into the sky, just as he was told to do.

Leviathan was taken by surprise. But instead of torturing Father John again, he leaped up to retrieve the box. He wanted to get if first before finishing him off.

Fr. John managed his way to the driver's seat. He pushed the boat as fast as she could go and tried heading for the Marine Corps base.

Leviathan grabbed the box. But to his astonishment, it was not what he expected. He quickly let it go, and the box fell into the Potomac River. He became weak and plunged back down to the water.

Beelzebul noticed from the water's edge that Leviathan could not touch the box. Then he realized someone else must have the other box. And he had a good idea who it was.

"Charles and Jean must have the box we need. Why haven't I heard from Vapula and Belial?" He tried to summon them but to no avail.

Leviathan managed to get back to Beelzebul to regain his strength.

"You fool! You had to waste valuable time trying to get stronger by torturing Fr. John. We might not have time to get the box we need. Go toward Powell Creek to stop Jean and Charles. Our other demons failed in their mission. Let's try and salvage the valuable time we have left," the master said.

With a vengeance, Leviathan moved through the river like lighting. Will Tobit be able to escape Leviathan's determination to retrieve the box? The demon knew now not to tease the humans before he gets the box. But he was unable to see his victim, thanks to Heather, Linda, and their company of angels. His power was not as strong after touching the wrong box. He began to slow down so he could try to find the boat Jean and Charles were on.

Beelzebul summoned all the dark angels he could.

"Michael! I know you are watching us. Come and show yourself! Why are these humans getting off so easy? I will have Leviathan cause the river to be so turbulent, your humans will not survive. We might not be able to see our victims, but we will comb this river until we get what we came for. My angels are ready for battle."

Michael appeared with his sword drawn. "Your threats are wasted on me, Satan. You want a battle? That is what you will get. But you will not get out humans today. The Spirit of God is with them, and they will not falter no matter how turbulent Leviathan makes the waters. You know why? Because Leviathan is not the creator of the water or the storms. So have your little outburst. There is no victory for you, but if you fight, then try your best. Our armies of angels outnumber yours. If you were wondering about Vapula and Belial, they have met their eternal punishment in hell. And when Jesus returns to this world, you and your dark angels will be cast into your eternal punishment as well."

Tobit was ready to be taken up to the heavens with the box. Heather warned everyone that Leviathan was coming.

But he had no idea where they were. Leviathan thought he had the power to control the waters, but he was not in control at all. He was surrounded by not only Heather and Linda's guardian angels, but Alexander was also summoned to join them with his fallen heroes. He put a strong fight but finally surrendered.

As Tobit was raised up to the heavens with the box of guilt in his hand, a whirlpool began to spin from the bottom of the river where the box of good deeds had fallen. It was sucked up into the whirlwind and was perfectly aligned with Tobit and the box of guilt. There was a bright light as though it was struck by lightning between the two. And as quickly as it had come, it vanished to the heavens.

*****

Sarah and Charles managed to survived the storms. They began to praise God and thank Him for witnessing His magnificent power. Their boat was tossed and had drifted away from where they were.

When they went to start the motor, it would not start. But they did drift toward the Marine Corps base.

Sarah noticed a smaller boat that was in worse condition than theirs. "Hello, is anyone on board? Charles, could you see if anyone is in that boat?"

Charles was close enough to see who was lying on the steering wheel. The waves in the river moved their boat close enough to toss a rope to it and pull themselves toward it.

"It is Father John! He must have lost consciousness. I will go aboard to see if I could revive him."

While on the Marine Corps base, Daymin, Nathan, and Nighjal were met by Maria and Robert. They all watched the event that went on in the Potomac River from shore. Nathan knew it was time to go out and bring back his son, Sarah, and Charles. Nathan spoke to everyone about his orders from the agency: "The agency has alerted the base police about an emergency on the Potomac River. We will meet the medical team at the pier to rescue someone on their boat because of the storm. We do know our agency is on this base too. This rescue will have to look like a normal rescue mission from an accident due to an act of nature. Yes, Maria, just like Jean and Tobit's accident; only this time, the outcome will give us back our loved ones."

Maria sighed. "Let's go and help save them from this natural disaster. This is one natural disaster I will not investigate."

All went aboard the police boat to rescue their brave friends. Finally, they reached the two battered boats. Sarah and Charles were on Father John's boat taking care of his wounds. They also had cuts and bruises, but theirs weren't as severe as Father John's who was tortured by Leviathan.

Nathan jumped on board and ran straight toward his son. "Please, medics, help him! It's going to be okay, John. We are here to help you."

Sarah ran to Maria. "You would have been so proud of your grandpop; now he is guarding our future. I am going to miss him. Every time I look up at the heavens, I will think of him."

Maria responded, "Yes, I am, Grandmom. Can I call you that now, or do I still have to call you Aunt Jean?"

Sarah answered, "Well, I am afraid that for now, it has to be Aunt Jean. Even though I think your mother might already know, this will have to be our secret for now

Maria sighed. "Oh, you know I am so grateful you are alive after all you have been through. I guess you are right. And you might have a legal problem pretending to be Jean."

Sarah smiled. "That is the least of my problems. We had a successful mission. We defeated our enemy and kept our country safe, at least for now. See, Maria, I said, "for now;" that means we are still needed. And that is why I have to be Jean. But in my heart, you will always be my precious granddaughter. I love you."

They were transported to the base hospital. Sarah and Charles were treated for their wounds and released. Father John was admitted and would stay there for a while. He drifted in and out of consciousness. Nathan was devastated to watch his son suffer so much.

He sat by his side along with his wife Michell, who arrived at the hospital as soon as she received the news from her husband.

"Nathan, why didn't you tell me what John was up to? I didn't even know he was a member of the agency."

He spoke in a soft voice, "Honestly, sweetheart, I did not know he was a member until yesterday. You were at your conference, and we had a short window to do this mission. The enemy was keeping an eye on everything we did; I could not communicate to anyone about our mission until it was completed. If I had called you about John, he might have been found out, and that just couldn't happen. God assured us everything would be okay."

Just before Michell could respond, Father John squeezed his mother's hand.

She looked over at him with tears in her eyes. "Son, why did you do this? We told you never to get involved with the secret agency."

Father John smiled at her. "I dedicated my life to Jesus. I am a man now, Mother. And please tell me, how I can say no to God? And, Father, didn't I tell you at the pulpit? 'Trust God for whatever mission He has for me.' I will be healed of my wounds soon enough.

You can be sure I will be ready to heed the call for my next mission, just as you both will be."

Nathan and Michell understood what their son was telling them. They all embraced each other and prayed a prayer of thanksgiving to the Lord.

Everyone stopped by to visit Father John before leaving the hospital. Maria asked him to bless them all before they headed for home. He began to share his feelings and pray for his loyal friends: "My dear friends and family, in such a short time, and even though we have known each other our whole lives, we came together as one to make the impossible possible. Thank God for his mighty angels: from the archangels down to the fallen heroes who have served not only our country but also the whole world; I feel their presence here with us now.

"I would like to quote from Psalm 103:20–22: 'Bless the Lord, all you Angels, mighty in strength and attentive, obedient to every command. Bless the Lord, all you hosts, ministers who do God's will. Bless the Lord, all creatures, everywhere in God's domain. Bless the Lord my soul!' God bless you all in the name of the Father, Son, and Holy Spirit."

Robert received a text from his grandfather.

> Please, Robert, tell all who are with you to come to our house before everyone goes their own way.

Robert clicked off his phone and said his goodbyes to Father John and thanked him for his blessing. One by one, they embraced the good priest and wished him a quick recovery.

Robert told everyone to drive to David and Casilda's cabin; David has invited everyone to come and celebrate their victory with them. All agreed except for Nathan and Michell; they wanted to stay with their son until he fully recovers.

Daymin and Nighjal took Nathan's van and offered to take Sarah and Charles with them to the cabin. Robert and Maria drove together in their car. When all arrived at the Figueiredos' estate, they were very tired and hungry. As soon as they knocked on the door, Casilda welcomed them in with the warmth of her hospitality. Their home had the aroma of freshly baked bread, and the table was filled with home cooking, which they all haven't had for a while. All had their fill and ready for a good night's sleep. The Figueiredo family had enough room for all of them to stay over and would send them off the next morning with a hearty breakfast.

Daymin, Nighjal, Robert, and Charles had quilts and sleeping bags in the large parlor which Casilda had set up for them. Maria and Sarah had their own room. And even though they were very tired, they managed to talk and share some needed time together.

Maria asked her grandmom, "Will you be going back to Maine?"

Sarah responded, "I am not sure. Charles and I want to get married soon. And I am leaving the choice of where we will live up to him. For now, I will go back, just to make up my mind and take in all that has happened in the past week. How about you and Robert?"

"Well, we have a lot to think about. I am thinking of asking if I can be stationed here at MCB Quantico. This is my last year in the Corps. And Robert was told he would be stationed here as well. And yes, we are going to get married too. But first, there is a little matter we have to take care of."

Sarah ended their conversation with a few words for Maria. "Yes, I know what that little matter is and God be with you both. Sleep tight, little Maria."

*****

Morning came. All had their fill of breakfast and said their farewells to David and Casilda and thanked them for all their prayers and hospitality. The last one who left was Robert.

He said to his grandparents, "You both mean the world to me. Maria and I will be back soon."

His gramps replied, "Yes, I know. And you two won't be visiting us alone. We will eagerly await her visit with you."

Robert never told his grandfather about what had happened with him and Maria all those years ago. He knew it was a sign from

God of what was to come. They embraced, and Robert went on his way.

*****

Maria and Robert were finally back at the Wright estate where their parents were waiting for them to come back. Before getting settled in and having the families gather around the table, Robert spoke to Maria's parents asking them for her hand in marriage. There was another question he had to ask as well.

"Mr. and Mrs. Thompson, I would like to make an offer on this property if you'll let me. There are many memories in this house from when it was the home of Maria's loving grandparents. I would like to share this with Maria if she accepts my proposal of marriage.

Now everyone was at the table.

He then turned toward Maria and got down on one knee. "Maria, would you please do me the honor of being my wife?'

She replied, "Yes, Robert. And the honor is all mine."

Robert just remembered something that Father John whispered to him before he boarded the boat the night before.

"Oh, Maria, I forget to tell you what Father John told me before his mission. He said it would be an honor for him to bless our marriage. He knew before I even asked you."

Gloria took Sarah aside and handed her an envelope. It contained Sarah's hair clippings from that night eight years ago.

The daughter whispered to her, "Mother, I love you, and I know you had to do what you had to do. You know a mother's intuition. I know you came back because of Maria's investigation. She is a clever little girl, the way she pretended she had to study for her test. I hope your new mission was successful. Your secret is always safe with me. Now, please give me a hug and let me whisper 'mommy' in your ear one more time."

Sarah was taken off guard. She could feel her husband smiling down at both of them.

She embraced her daughter and whispered back to her, "Please, precious little girl, call me mommy. I love you more than you could ever imagine."

Then she thought to herself, *Tobit was right. She did know for all these years.*

Maria looked over at them both and smiled.

*****

Months have gone by. Robert had settled into his new house with his wife, Maria. Sarah and Charles were also married, and they lived in the secret hideaway which they rebuilt into a comfortable home.

Robert and Maria were also reunited with their daughter, Sarah. The couple who adopted Maria's baby as an infant let Maria name her, so she named her after her grandmom. Maria had been contacted by an adoption agency. It so happened that Sarah's adoptive parents died in a fatal car accident. With the help of a few fallen heroes and Saint Michael, the agency found out about her real parents. Now they are all happy together.

Maria had made it her mission to find the truth behind her grandparents' untimely death only to find out that one grandparent survived. But it was a secret to everyone else. She discovered her grandfather's world within the Secret Service of Angels which she now belonged to along with her husband Robert.

About the Author

Mary "Fig" Stearne was born and raised in Philadelphia, Pennsylvania, to loving parents who taught her right from wrong. She went to a Catholic school and learned about Jesus and fell in love. During her teenage years in the late '60s and early '70s, she was caught up with the flower power phase. Thank God for His patience and mercy; she came to her senses and asked for forgiveness, and now she is on a long journey of doing His will. She doesn't claim perfection yet, but that day will come when she will meet Jesus face to face.

God has blessed her with a wonderful husband and three beautiful girls who are now women, but in her eyes, they will always be her little girls. They have given her ten precious grandchildren, of which she is extremely over the top in love with.

She wrote this novel because she wanted to let people be aware that Satan is out there, and he is trying to take hold of our souls. She wants her audience to know that you can fight back with prayer and commitment. She believes that having a personal relationship with Jesus is the answer.

She loves a good mystery, and that is why she decided to write this fictional mystery with a twist of truth.

CPSIA information can be obtained
at www.ICGtesting.com
Printed in the USA
BVHW080142221021
619246BV00001B/5